In an Uncharted Country

In an Uncharted Country

stories by

Clifford Garstang

[handwritten inscription: 4/16/10 — For Craig & Ault — Thanks so much for joining me on this journey. I hope you enjoy! CliffGarstang]

Press 53
Winston-Salem, NC

Press 53
PO Box 30314
Winston-Salem, NC 27130

First Edition

Cover design by Kevin Watson

Cover photo, "Farm Implements," copyright © 2009 by Robert Miller

Printed on acid-free paper

ISBN: 978-0-9824416-7-1

for my parents

Contents

Acknowledgments

The author wishes to acknowledge these fine publications where the following stories have appeared:

"Flood, 1978" appeared in *The Circle Magazine* and *Eureka Literary Magazine*

"Saving Melissa" appeared in *The Ledge*

"William & Frederick" appeared in *North Dakota Quarterly* and *R-KV-R-Y* as "Leviathan"

"The Clattering of Bones" appeared in *Timber Creek Review* and *R-KV-R-Y*

"White Swans" appeared in *The Hub* as "The White Swan"

"Savage Source" appeared in *Ashé Journal*

"Hand-painted Angel" appeared in *Bellowing Ark*

"In an Uncharted Country" appeared in *RE:AL*

"The Nymph and the Woodsman" appeared in *Whitefish Review*

"Heading for Home" appeared in *The Baltimore Review*

"Stonewall" appeared in *Confluence*

FLOOD, 1978

The night is hushed, except for snow tickling the dark windows. I hear Pop shuffle into the kitchen. A pan bangs on the stove. He'd said he'd warm up that broth for Alice, in case she feels like eating something when she stirs. He's always taken real good care of my Alice. Ever since the flood.

Pop's 83 now, so I guess he was in his fifties the year the flood washed out the bridge. We'd had mountains of snow already that winter—started around Thanksgiving and was still coming down on Valentine's Day. That was the big storm, close to two feet all at once it seemed, *whump*, on top of the foot we already had. Pop and me made loads of extra cash plowing. About the time we'd finish with our regulars, along'd come another blizzard and we'd start all over again. By February everybody was sick of it, but we figured maybe this one was the end. So we all just watched it fall, pile up on the shed, build drifts against the junipers. There's an old woman who lives in this county and paints pictures of barns and old houses and whatnot in all the seasons, and this looked just like one of her paintings.

I have to tell you something about Pop. He worked like a hound his whole life, scraping up enough to buy this farm and move him and Momma out here. That's when the work really started, though. And it never was enough—had to take jobs in town, too, or they'd have lost the place. Then they had us kids, me and my sister, Irene, and Teddy who was always sickly and who we buried just shy of his tenth birthday. Never was easy, with school and clothes and doctors. Except when he was giving orders—mow this pasture, start planting the beans, don't forget to bring in the cows—or when we sat down to Sunday dinner, I hardly ever saw him back then. Now Pop's an old man, stooped and gray. He could just sit and let other folks do it all. But he won't do that. Has to be working at something all the time. Been a big help, too, especially now with Alice sickly.

Pop's spry enough to do some of the cleaning, and if he didn't tend the garden we just wouldn't have one. There's no way we could use all the tomatoes and beans and everything he coaxed out of that red clay last summer. It was Alice used to do the canning and such, and Momma before her. Me and Pop don't have what it takes for that kind of work. Plus, with the boys grown, we don't need as much as we used to. But Pop keeps at it.

"Pop," I tell him, "it's a waste. Stuff'll rot on the vine."

"You never know, boy," he says, and I'm not quite sure what he means. I've got grown sons, one with a family of his own, and I'll always be "boy" to Pop.

Anyway, back during that snowstorm, me and Alice were sitting at the kitchen table, drinking our coffee, Momma at the sink drying dishes even though the doctor'd told her to stay off her feet, the dizzy spells and headaches coming too often for his liking, and we were staring out the window, dreamlike, at that snow sailing down, fluffing up in pillows on the pine branches, turning the creek black with cold. Pop was down in the cellar hammering at something or other, whistling, never happier than when his hands were going.

"Sit down, Mother," Alice said. "Let me finish that." She meant it, too—had the dishtowel in her hand, ready to go if just this once Momma would give in.

"No, dear," Momma said. "You're exhausted. Enjoy a little peace." She knew Alice had been up with Timmy in the night, one of those bad dreams little boys will have. Alice sighed and dropped the towel on the counter, sat back down with me.

The boys couldn't go to school, of course, and no point in me trying to get down to the warehouse. I was just starting out in those days, after the Army, which was why me and Alice and the boys lived with my folks. Alice loved Momma and Pop. They loved her, too, couldn't help but, with her easy grin and being prone to break into song on a pretty day. Most of the time things were good. But Alice was antsy for us to move out on our own, even if it meant living in a shack, like some folks do. I was torn, to tell the truth, but I had to take her side.

"We're going to look for a place," I said to Pop while the two of us were hanging a new stock gate. There was no place to hide from the sun and sweat poured off my cheeks. Pop wore a beat-up hat with a crushed brim.

"She put you up to this, boy? Because you got to make your own decisions."

"It's my decision, Pop."

"Won't set well with your mother," he said. Which meant, as far as I could tell, that he didn't approve, and expected me to abide by his judgment. We went on, and I said no more.

At the time of that big snow, Pop was still working, and since he was around that morning he must've figured it was going to be impossible to get to the lumberyard, even if they were open, which more'n likely they were not. Mind I said impossible, because if it was just going to be damn hard, Pop would've gone ahead and tried. Probably would've made it, too.

After that dreamy morning, we all found things to keep ourselves busy. Momma and Alice cooked up a storm, baking pies and fixing a big roast for supper. Alice taught the boys how to cut out construction paper Valentines to take to school. I helped Pop in his workshop. It seemed like a good time to try again about me and Alice and the kids getting our own place, but I didn't know how. The snow made everything so peaceful, and to tell the truth it had been a long time since the old man and me had done anything together that wasn't back-breaking work. I didn't want to disturb that. We tightened up a wobbly dining room chair, then built a little bookshelf for the boys' room that we painted a deep blue to match the old dresser we'd refinished a couple months back. They loved the shelf when we finished it. Couldn't wait to fill it up. I remember that blue, the color of the glass Momma collected, those bowls and goblets we still have.

Alice wouldn't let the boys outside by themselves in that blizzard, but by afternoon they were wild—stir-crazy Momma called it—so Alice bundled them up in mittens and boots and their heavy wool jackets, and I took them out, me and Bosco, the happiest little chocolate Lab you'd ever want to know. Me and Timmy and Teddy, named for my brother that died, of course, the three of us wore that poor pup out throwing snowballs for him to chase, only to have them crumble and disappear in his mouth. Drove him batty trying to figure out where they went. The boys had a blast, and we all came in, Bosco too, cold and tired and ready to sit by the fire and listen to the wind howl.

By the second day, when the snow finally stopped, Pop and I started plowing. We plowed all afternoon and I kept on the next morning when Pop finally made it to work, then I had to head off, too, for a shift at the warehouse. With the roads mostly clear by then, even the schools reopened and the boys had to go, no matter how much they whined. I didn't see anything wrong with a couple of little kids staying home from first grade an extra day to enjoy the snow, but Pop thought I needed to teach them about responsibility, about showing up no matter what.

"Won't be no good as men if they don't take the punches now," Pop said. He'd said that same thing when I was a kid, just like, when my little brother died, he said men had to be strong, no softies allowed. That's not how I wanted to raise my boys. Made me more determined than ever to move out.

Next day, Momma didn't get out of bed till after Pop left for work, which was real late for her, and Alice told me Momma took a nap that afternoon, which she almost never did. "Just a little under the weather," Momma said when I asked how she was feeling that night. She smiled like she'd made a joke.

A couple days after that storm—three feet of snow on the ground and more on the trees and roof—a warm spell set in. You could hear the creek pick up pace a little—suddenly loud, like somebody cranked up the volume—and snowmelt trickled steadily in the gutters and drainpipes. The sun showed up for a day, and that big, snowy dune turned to slop. When the clouds came back, I figured the weather would turn cold again and we'd have another blizzard. But it stayed warm, and started to rain. Drizzled all night long, couldn't even hear it, but if you turned on a light you'd see it misting the windows. Still that way when we got up—foggy, like a damp rag set on top of us.

Alice dressed the boys for school, packed lunches in their tin boxes, and hurried them outside when the bus came. Momma still felt poorly. Pop had already set off for the lumberyard and I was fixing to head out, too, filling in for a buddy on his day shift, happy for the extra hours. The rain came down heavier, and the only thing I could think of was how much snow that would be if it was colder, and how glad I was to see rain instead. Didn't want to see another flake of the white stuff for a long time.

I drove off in a downpour. As I crossed the bridge on Sparksburg Pike that goes over the creek, the only way out of our hollow, I had a feeling there was going to be a problem. The creek was already high from the melt, and that heavy rain and all the snow still on the ground spelled trouble. Thank goodness our house was on a rise. Folks who lived down low were in for wet times. That Coffey family, Dean and Janet and their kids, had a trailer just about on top of that creek and I hoped they had got themselves to higher ground. Rained all day. I heard on the radio at work they looked for three, maybe four, inches before it was over. And the weather stayed warm. That's what really set us up.

In the middle of the afternoon, Sam Poole—a bald fireplug who'd been shift manager long as any of the guys could remember—signaled me up to his office, said I had a call. I never got calls. We weren't supposed to use the phone except in an emergency, so I knew something was up. First thing I thought about was the boys. Something over at the school. With all that snow on a flat roof, and the rain, it could be a problem. My neck got cold and then it spread down my back and started me shaking. I don't pray much, but I prayed then. Please, God, don't let anything happen to the boys. I remembered what it was like with my little brother, and I didn't think I could take it.

"Hank, it's me," said Alice. I calmed right down, because there was no panic in her voice. If it was the boys, she wouldn't have been able to speak at all, much less like she was calling just to chitchat.

"What's wrong, honey?" I saw Sam looking at me, pretending like he wasn't paying attention.

"It's the bridge. It's gone."

"It was there when I came in."

"Irene called and I just drove down there to see. It's clean washed away."

"Jesus."

"They're keeping the boys at school until you can get them. You and Pop'll have to stay in town—Irene's expecting you."

"You and Momma okay?"

"We're fine. Except . . ."

"Except what?"

"Momma doesn't feel well. Worried about the boys, I guess."

I picked the boys up at school. When they saw me pull up they both ran out and grabbed me by the legs. The littler one, Timmy, was in tears, flushed cheeks to match the red sweater we'd put him in that morning. His teacher, Mrs. Meyer, said he'd tried to get on the bus to go home, and when she pulled him and Teddy off he flew into a rage. "I want to go home," he kept yelling. Can't blame him. I wanted to go home, too. Teddy was not quite as worked up. A year older than Timmy, his blond curls a shade darker, he looked like he was close to tears himself, but wanted to act like a big boy. I tried to phone the house to tell Alice the boys were okay, but by then the line was dead.

It was still raining like mad. Already recovered, the boys hopped into my truck, talking a blue streak about the rain and the bridge and how Mrs. Meyer came on the bus and told them to get off and the Bell kids, all five of them, wouldn't budge, didn't believe the teacher.

"Those stupid Bells," Timmy said.

Truth was, I didn't believe it either. I'd lived out Sparksburg Pike my whole life, more than 30 years, and that bridge had always been there, and there'd been floods before, so how could it just disappear one afternoon? Didn't make sense. And I wasn't keen on spending the night, or however long it was going to be, at my sister's. Pop and Irene hadn't gotten along too well, didn't even speak, as far as I knew, not since she married that Catholic fella, Marvin. And Irene never did cotton much to the boys, loud and boisterous as they could be. I guess you could say she and I were on the outs, too. Just didn't sound like much fun. So we didn't go there.

We drove to the bridge.

We weren't the only ones, not by a long shot. Soon as we got close, we were in a traffic jam with an assortment of old pickups, like they were waiting for the light to change. Because the bridge truly was gone, I could see that now. I told the boys to stay put, but I got out and joined the crowd at the edge of the creek, right where the bridge used to be. Pop was there, too, and some of our neighbors, all of us standing in the rain like we were at some hard-luck picnic. Some of the other folks were just gawkers. I didn't know them, and after a while they pulled their trucks out of line and went back the other way.

That bridge was something. It had crossed the creek on cement pilings, like stepping-stones connected by arches. In normal high water those arches let the creek flow without doing any harm. But this wasn't normal high water. The creek was up near the level of the road, which meant it had to be more than 15 feet, and flying. While we stood there, a telephone pole shot our way, whipped on the water like one of Timmy's toy boats, smack onto the bank, sending up a spray that chased folks back from the edge. Then a stump came sailing down, crashed through the rapids just upstream from where the bridge used to be and zoomed past. About the size of a coffin it was—I had to look twice to see if maybe it wasn't, but as it churned I saw it had a tangle of roots at one end. That's what must've happened. A few of those logs bombard the pilings, and maybe a river that wild could dislodge a boulder or two and send them tumbling, too, and pretty quick that bridge'd start to melt away like snow. And when it gave up just a little of its strength, the river would take the rest. Probably didn't take long.

"How we getting home, boy?" Pop asked.

"Alice says we're to stay with Irene. All arranged."

He rolled his eyes and spat into the river. "I'm going home."

"That'll be interesting to watch. You never were much of a swimmer."

Pop paced along the edge, where the tender asphalt dripped away, cinder by cinder, like he was looking for a place to cross. I stood back and watched—it wouldn't do any good to get in his way. The sheriff had shown up by then. He tugged Pop from the edge, said they'd already pulled some folks from the water downstream and he wasn't keen on jumping in after anybody himself. Pop shuffled back to where I stood and looked across the creek toward where our house was, behind a couple of hills.

"Boy, something's wrong."

"Yes, sir. That bridge is what's wrong."

"At home. We got to get home."

The creek was raging and the rain was still pouring and I could barely hear Pop's voice, but the way he looked at me direct instead of off to the side or down at the ground like he did when he thought he might be saying something foolish, I could tell he was serious and I was not to oppose him. His jaw was set, and he really got me worried when he grabbed my arm and said, "We got to get to your Momma."

"Pop, I got the boys with me." As soon as I said that I remembered they were alone and probably scared. I ran back to the truck and sure enough both the boys were sniffling and it smelled like maybe Timmy'd had an accident. They whined about the rain when I pulled them out of the truck and Timmy's sniffles turned into bawling when I bumped his knee on the door. Tears streamed out of Teddy's eyes, too, but I saw by the way he was holding his breath that he was trying to stop. I had them both in my arms, and

ran up to the Albertsons' Olds and rapped on the roof. Ben rolled
his window down partway.

"Quite an armful you got there, Hank," Ben said. Ethel leaned
across the seat and smiled at the boys. She's a grandmother herself,
great with kids.

"Thing is, Ben, I got to help Pop with something and we need
to get the boys over to my sister's place. You're not getting home
anytime soon, I reckon. Would you mind running them back there?
I hate to ask."

Ethel leaned across again. "No problem at all, honey. We were
just saying we need to go find a place for ourselves, probably stay at
that motel right there near Irene's. No problem at all."

I settled the boys in the back of Ben's big Ninety-Eight, warned
them not to touch the power window button, apologized again to
Ben and Ethel for imposing, and especially for the stink Timmy
had about him. I kissed each boy on the forehead and tickled both
in the ribs to see if I could start them laughing.

"You boys be good," I said.

Ethel had found a roll of Lifesavers in her purse and the boys
seemed torn between being worried that their daddy was leaving
and making sure they got their favorites, cherry for Teddy, lime for
Timmy. I was able to get that door shut without too much of a
fuss. Good folks, those Albertsons.

I jockeyed my truck off the road, then found Pop behind the
wheel of his. He didn't say anything, just looked straight ahead. We
swung around and turned on Route 320. I saw what he had in
mind—there weren't a lot of options. All the same, it seemed
foolhardy. We'd follow along the creek a ways, till the next bridge,
maybe ten miles upstream, and pray it hadn't been washed out, too.
Prayer was part of Pop's plan for sure. On the other side of the
creek, the mountain shot almost straight up, and what we were
going to have to do was drive over that mountain, road or no road.

We slogged on, wipers making a racket, splashing and scraping
across the windshield. I didn't spend a lot of time in Pop's truck so
I hadn't noticed it before, but a crack ran the length of that

windshield, winding and twisting like some crazy river. Soon that other bridge was just ahead, some trucks and a car stopped to one side, like before. But Pop's prayers had been answered because that bridge was still standing. Creek water sheeted across the top, but at least it was there. A deputy was setting up a sawhorse barricade and we drove right up to it and that deputy came around to Pop's side. Pop still had his hand on the shift when he rolled down his window. Rain poured off the man's hat and slicker.

"We got to get through," Pop said, matter-of-fact.

"Well, sir, you can't do that. Maybe you saw that bridge out a ways back and this one's fixing to do the same. Ain't safe."

Right then, looking straight into the man's eyes, Pop slipped the truck into gear and gunned forward, smashed that barricade, and we about flew through the water on that bridge. I don't think we could've stopped even if Pop had wanted to, which he surely did not. I turned around and saw that deputy shaking his head, and the folks in those other trucks were cheering and clapping. I'll never forget the look on Pop's face, though, determined like I'd never seen him before.

That bridge was only part of the problem, of course. We went on down the road and came to one turnoff and Pop slowed, but then kept going, like he had an idea what he was looking for and that wasn't it. He did that one more time and then we came to a third turn, a gravel track between fenced pastures, and he turned in without hesitating a lick. We splashed along, bouncing through puddles bigger than some ponds we'd fished when I was growing up, spinning tires in muddy ruts. Soon we were heading uphill, and there was still snow cover on the track, not so much mud. It was starting to get dark.

I'd never been up that way before. We went by an old wreck of a house, windows broke, roof caved in, and Pop named the folks who used to live there. Couldn't make a go of it and moved out when I was a kid.

"Good hunting up here," Pop said, about the last thing he said the whole rest of the way.

The road stopped, but Pop drove right on into pasture. Tearing through the snow and high grass, he leaned over the steering wheel. I leaned, too, looking out for rocks and stumps and whatnot. Pop didn't seem surprised when we came to another track, an old logging road maybe, and that took us right over the top of the mountain. We started down again, faster of course, dark or not.

At that point I knew more or less where we were and I began to wonder what we'd find when we got home. Something had spooked Pop. Momma must have been sicker than I knew, was what I figured. I wondered about the boys, too, but they were in good hands, between Ethel Albertson and Irene. Anyway, we kept crashing down that mountain, the springs in the seat squeaking and us bouncing up and down and the shocks in that truck taking a terrible beating.

"Tree," I yelled. Pop swerved, slammed on the brakes, and if that tree hadn't been there, leaning across the trail, we might've flipped. As it was, Pop hit it broadside and it banged in his door, smashed his window to pieces. Pop sat there, hands on the steering wheel like he was just waiting for traffic to clear, glass all over his lap and the door pushed in against his knee, rain splattering his arm. I got out and levered the tree out of the way. Pop was tapping his thumbs on the wheel like he might be thinking, "Hurry it up, boy." I ran around to my side and jumped in.

That logging track started heading off in the wrong direction, away from our place, so Pop steered off-road again. It must have been killing him, but he slowed some. Wasn't only rocks and trees worried me, but those hills were scarred with mighty steep drops, even abandoned quarries that could appear under us from nowhere. We were so far back in those hills, if we fell into a hole like that we'd never be found. Period.

I didn't see it coming, but we ran smack into a boulder. Good thing we weren't moving any faster or we'd both have flown through that cracked windshield. Pop tried to back up, but when I hopped out I saw how tore up the front was, that rock knifed into the hood and the engine block smashed. That truck wasn't going nowhere.

Pop's calm slipped off him like he'd shed his skin. "Dammit," he said, "Goddammit," cursing like I never heard him. He kicked the tire and slammed his hand against the fender and of course that did no good. I jumped over to him and saw tears snaking down his craggy face. He was having trouble breathing, too.

"Come on, Pop. We'll cut across the Bell place and be home before you know it. Okay?" He couldn't answer me, though, just nodded. We took off, left that truck right where it was. Still there to this day.

We had to climb more fences than I remembered there were, but finally we spotted the house. A faint light flickered in the downstairs windows and Pop took off running when we saw that. I had to hoof it to keep up.

He pushed open the front door and ran in, muddy boots and all. Momma was lying on the sofa, Alice perched on the floor next to her, holding her hand, stroking her arm, a soft glow over both of them from the candles they'd lit. The sight made us both stop, like that truck on the boulder. Alice looked up at us and moved out of the way. Pop knelt in her place, took up Momma's hand, laid his arm across her like they were dancing. I shuffled in to stand behind Pop so I could look down on Momma, and she must've heard me. She opened her eyes, and a weak smile came on her face.

"We'll get you to a doctor," Pop said, in that thin voice he used sometimes when he was sick, or feeling thankful, like grace before supper. Momma nodded, barely. She must've known what it took for Pop and me to get home, and knew plain as day it would take a miracle to get her to the hospital. Maybe I could've run down to where the bridge used to be and somehow got the folks on the other side to understand, and maybe one of them could've called somebody, if any phones anywhere worked, and maybe a helicopter could've landed in the soupy rain and taken her off. Somehow I knew there wasn't time for all that.

And there wasn't. Pop held her hand, Alice and I were right behind him, gripping each other, and the candles flickered when the wind gusted outside. Rain tapped on the windows. Momma closed her eyes and was gone.

Pop cried, hard sobs, and lifted her hand to his face. He knelt there for the longest time. Finally I got down on my knees with him and put my arms around him, Alice did the same, and he let us do it. I loved Momma, too, of course, but I couldn't really know what Pop was feeling, way beyond loss, or grief. Not then.

The snow's stopped, and the wind's died down some. Alice whispers my name. In the shadows, she peers at me from her pillow, and I go to her side. With her like this, I'm a kid lost in the dark, and can't find my way. Everything hits me. Now I'm holding on to her, tears streaming down my face, and I can feel her ebb away. Not all at once, but a breath at a time.

When it's over, Pop's right there. He leans over and kisses her brow. He puts his arm around me. He presses my head on his shoulder, and lets me weep.

SAVING MELISSA

The rain fell hard, sheeting down my windshield, noon sky dark, clouds rumbling. It was a chilly June: Melissa not in school, playing sweetly on the farmhouse porch with that one Barbie Max let her keep, one I gave her, on her chubby knees, glancing up now and then trying not to fear the thunder. The new wife slept inside, in my bed, or chopped onions in my kitchen, sipped tea from my wedding china. Paid no attention to the child. My child.

I opened the door of the Cutlass and popped the mottled umbrella—two spokes bent. Melissa lifted her eyes, got up one leg at a time, and watched me. She peeked into the house; her ponytail bobbed; she looked back and took a tentative step. She knew I wasn't supposed to be there. The judge had said so, had said right in front of everybody her mommy wasn't fit. Barbie dangled by her ankles. Melissa took another step, to the gray edge of the porch.

Then I ran, splashing across the muddy road, up the drive, one eye on the farmhouse door. Melissa smiled—a tooth missing. I hugged her tight, kissed her, dashed with her through the rain, strapped her in back, and we were on our way.

As I drove, I sang God's praises for bringing my dear girl back to me, and rescuing us from Max. At first, we sang the hymns together, loud and strong, "A mighty fortress is our God, a bulwark never failing." Melissa didn't know all the words, but she hummed along or waved her hands like the church choir director. Then she stopped and slumped down to where I could barely see her in the mirror. I quit the hymns and thought the radio might distract her. But we hadn't gone more than twenty miles, no further west than Highland County, our backs to the Blue Ridge and just climbing the Alleghenies, my country station edging into hoarseness, when she started to whimper.

"I want to go home," Melissa said. I'm hungry, I'm thirsty, I want Barbie. Barbie had fallen to the porch when I grabbed her, too frantic to worry about such a small thing. Tears sprouted on her rosy cheeks, first sign of a good wail. I didn't think I could handle one of her tantrums just then. Gritting my teeth, I slapped the front seat.

"Stop it," I said. My voice was loud, not quite shouting. In the mirror, I saw her face tighten with surprise, more tears.

"We'll get you a new Barbie, honey," I said, softening. Anything to stop the crying. "Lots of Barbies. I promise."

Sobs gave way to sniffles. "Are we going to see Daddy?"

Of course she missed her father—those strong, welcoming arms, comfortable warm flannel, the familiar smells of tobacco and tractor fuel.

"No, sweetie. We don't want to see Daddy, do we? He's a bad man. He hurt us. He hurt you."

"No, he didn't."

"I won't let him hurt you anymore." He had. He must have, and she needed to believe it. He took everything from me. I was taking it back.

Seven years ago that was, Melissa just eight. The farm hasn't changed much. Baskets of gaudy geraniums still hang on the sagging porch; the boxwoods are higher, almost up to the railing; phlox borders the walk. The barn needs painting.

That Cutlass is long gone. I sit in the gray Toyota I bought out in Arizona, windshield cracked, parked down the road so they won't notice. It's raining sheets again, just like the day we left. That seems to fit, somehow, makes everything right, like it never happened, like Melissa's up there on that porch same as before, like time stood still.

***

I knew Max would try to find us—her. Wouldn't have been any doubt in his mind what happened. If Melissa was missing, Mona took her. Max blamed me for everything.

"You're a menace, Mona," Max had said that time Melissa fell off the porch and twisted her ankle. For a while we'd thought it was broken. "How hard can it be to watch the child?"

"I didn't do it," I said, whining. We'd been dancing, spinning frantically, laughing. Melissa shrieked when she went over the edge. "I didn't do it on purpose."

Always it was my fault, to hear Max tell it, even before the divorce and the lopsided custody mess. Still makes my face hot to think about it, all these years later, Max standing there in his shiny brown suit and skinny tie, talking about me like I wasn't even there. How could they do that to me? Pills, Doris said she found in the medicine chest. Of course there were pills—who doesn't take pills? And me with the bad back ever since my first accident. Reckless, Max said, sore about the damage I'd done to his precious Oldsmobile. Unfit, they all said. Supervised visitation, the judge said, softly, like he was ashamed of himself, taking a child from her mother.

So we had to get away. I couldn't let them take her from me, could I? Couldn't let sweet Melissa stay in a place like that, with the Godless lies and hate?

I hadn't planned to go far—just to Momma's up in the hills, to wait, to see what would happen, to make folks realize I wasn't a bad mother, that Max had twisted everything. Then we could come back, Melissa would live with me, and we'd have a fresh start. But we drove and drove and Melissa whimpered and I realized we couldn't stay at Momma's, even if she wanted us, which she wouldn't. We'd be in the way—it was such a small trailer. Momma's temper would flare, like when I was little. Besides, it was the first place he'd look.

We slept in the car mostly, which, for a while, was a treat for Melissa, and washed up in filling stations. We ate at McDonald's for the first couple of days. It kept Melissa happy, but I saw how quickly my cash would disappear, so I bought bread and cheese slices at a 7-11 and we had sandwiches after that, until Melissa saw a green spot on the crust. She yelled like I'd slapped her, not knowing what it was. We couldn't just throw it away, I told her. I showed her how to pick the mold off and bite around it, but she wouldn't eat—not until her hunger took over. That's how I learned, too, just about her age. That's just the way it was, nobody's fault.

Once I'd changed my mind about going to Momma's, and it hit me we couldn't ever go back home, I didn't have any kind of a plan, other than to just keep going, get as far away from Max as I could. And that's what we did, until the day we ran out of money. If I'd needed to use a payphone I couldn't have done it. We were low on gas besides, the telltale Shell card long since abandoned.

"Mommy," Melissa said, "I'm hungry." I watched her gnaw on the end of her pony tail and didn't stop her. If we'd had any, she would've eaten moldy bread.

"I know, honey. Mommy's got to think." We were in Ohio, and without divine intervention we weren't going another mile. I'd pulled to the curb on a busy, dusty road, just shy of what looked to be that town's only stoplight. And across the street was a grocery store, not a supermarket or anything like that, just a little thing with bruised fruit piled in the front window and a rack of bread towering over the cash register.

"Stay here, honey. Mommy'll be right back."

I had to wait for a car to pass, and then a semi rig, before I could bolt across. Gave me just enough time to think what to do.

A gray-haired woman perched on a stool, a crossword puzzle book open in front of her on a glass countertop that preserved yellowed news clippings, an obituary, bounced checks—like a kid's butterfly collection.

"Can I help you?" The woman marked her place with a stubby yellow pencil.

"Just need to pick up a few things," I said, practically sang, my smile as big as I could muster. "For my daughter. Out there in the car?" I pointed. When the woman craned her neck to look around the fruit baskets toward the Cutlass, I grabbed a loaf of bread, nearly let it slip out of my sweaty hands, and held it behind my back.

"Pretty little gal," said the woman. "Passing through?"

"That's right," I said, making a show of looking around the store, all the while hiding that bread. "You don't have any Pepto-Bismol do you? Her stomach's been kind of queasy." The woman shook her head. I don't know what I'd have done if she'd had some—I knew as soon as I said it I should have asked for something more peculiar. "I guess there's nothing else I need then. Thank you kindly." And I backed out the door.

"It's just bread, Mommy," Melissa said when I jumped in the car, brandishing the loaf like we'd won a prize.

"Hush, baby. It'll have to do."

In the next town I managed to snag a jar of Skippy and a warm bottle of Coke. Melissa thought spreading the peanut butter on the squishy bread with her finger was great fun, for which I said a little prayer. She was sound asleep when I pulled away from a Marathon station without paying for the gas I'd pumped. And she was still out when I ran back to the car, breathless, after grabbing a wad of bills from the cash register of an all-night restaurant somewhere in Indiana.

Distance changes everything. Perspective. Memory. Truth. By the time we got to Iowa it didn't seem quite so needful to run, like we were safe there. Like Max would forget. So we stopped. Muscatine, Iowa. I found work in a diner on the town square, even rented a room for no money down in a nice house, belonged to a customer, a widow who was just what I thought other people's mothers must be like—plump, tidy, smelling of bath powder.

Miss Eleanor—that's what she wanted Melissa to call her and it stuck on my tongue, too—seemed to enjoy having us around, least that's what they said at the diner. So we settled in, Melissa and me, except now my name was Julia, after that pretty actress with the big laugh I liked so much, and a new last name, too. Lost my driver's license when my wallet was stolen, I told people; Miss Eleanor helped me out there, and talked to her cousin at the DMV who got me a new one, with my new name. I was surprised it was that easy, but folks didn't have any reason to doubt me, so they cut a few corners just to be neighborly. I tried to get Melissa to start calling herself something different, too—Elizabeth.

"So pretty," I said. "Who wouldn't want to be called Elizabeth?"

"Why I can't I be Melissa anymore?" she asked, and I couldn't stand her blubbering so I just let it be.

After only a month, the Darvon ran out. A day without it and my head felt like it was being ripped in two; my back ached worse than ever. Melissa asked me to braid her hair and my hands just shook. I couldn't do it. I shouted at her, like it was her doing, and that made her cry for her Daddy, which made my head hurt worse. The pharmacy wouldn't give me a refill, of course, with the name being wrong, and the quack I saw about a new prescription took one look at my eyes and jumpy hands and turned me down flat, launched into a lecture about painkillers being worse than liquor. I begged him, but he wouldn't budge. Finally, Miss Eleanor came to the rescue again and smooth-talked her doctor, a handsome older gentleman with soft hands and a warm smile. He listened to my story about the accident—in Kentucky, I told him, where we had relatives—and warned me about the pills being habit-forming, all the while writing out the prescription in his easy scrawl.

As settled as our life got, I was never sure what lengths Max would go to. I thought about letting Momma know where we were, but I was afraid she'd write it down somewhere, maybe send Melissa a card on her birthday, and Max would find out. So we called her now and then, not too often, short calls in case they were listening.

"Momma?" I whispered into the payphone at the back of the diner, the first time I called. The clank of dishes in the kitchen made it hard to hear, and there was a sickly sweet smell drifting from the restrooms.

"Is that you, Mona? My land, what trouble you've caused!"

"I've missed you, Momma."

"Mona, it's a foolish thing you've done."

I was careful not to say anything about being in Iowa. I even let

slip we were in Florida, to throw them off the scent if they were
still chasing us. At the time, I didn't know you could trace where a
person was calling from. If I did, I wouldn't have phoned at all.

"It's me, Momma," I said another time.

"Mona, honey, Max is worried sick about Melissa."

"I can take care of her, Momma." I thought I heard something
in the background, voices maybe, or a whirring fan.

"But what kind of life is it for the child? Don't be stupid, honey.
You'd best come on home. A girl needs her father."

I hung up, and didn't call much after that.

One day I came home from the diner and Melissa was on the
phone, her hand over the dial like she was trying to remember the
number.

"Who are you calling, sweetie?" I asked.

"Daddy." She started to dial.

I snatched the phone out of her hand, dropped it back in the
cradle and grabbed her by the arms. "We can't call Daddy, baby. He
doesn't want to talk to us anymore. Remember?" I'd told her he
moved, that the old number wouldn't work, that he'd punish us
both if he found us. She sniffed and nodded.

After we'd been in Muscatine for nearly a year—Melissa content
in the third grade and Miss Eleanor beginning to feel like family,
more like an aunt we'd moved in with than a perfect stranger—
Tommy Carr walked into the diner one morning at the tail end of
the breakfast rush. I knew him right off. Hadn't we been in chorus
together senior year? I spilled the coffee I was pouring as I watched
him shuffle in and look around, not sure where to go, until he
plopped into a booth. Not my station, thank God, but I still couldn't
risk it. I mopped up my mess with a fistful of napkins, told the
cook I wasn't feeling good, which was the truth, and hid in the
pantry until Tommy paid his check and left. What was he doing
there, in my diner, a thousand miles from home?

And what if he saw me? He'd get back and bump into Max at
the Elks, and he'd say, "You'll never guess who I ran into, in Iowa
of all places," and Max'd have the cops there in a minute.

I went right home after my shift, a crazy afternoon when my back felt like I had a knife stuck in me, told Miss Eleanor there'd been a death in the family, and started to pack up what little we had. God bless her, she didn't ask questions, just put the kettle on for tea. Melissa was no help, trying to pull things out of the suitcase as fast I put them in, shouting that she didn't want to leave. She had school. She had friends.

Finally, I had to slap her. She stopped. Her eyes stretched wide. "I don't need this," I yelled.

"I hate you," she screamed, edging away, her hand covering her hot cheek, as if she needed to hide what I'd done. "I hate you! I hate you! I hate you!" She ran to the bathroom and the lock banged into place. I heard her sob as she slumped to the floor.

I finished packing and loaded the Cutlass. Miss Eleanor busied herself in the kitchen, making us sandwiches for the trip. Then it was time. I tiptoed down the hall to the bathroom.

"Honey," I whispered through the door. "We have to go. I'll make it up to you, I promise."

"I want to go home," she said, snuffling. "I want Daddy."

The hallway was dark, the ceiling fixture missing its bulb. I put my palm to the door.

"We can't go home," I said. The door was warm against my hand. I felt the varnish crack under my fingers. I listened for Melissa's breathing. "Your father's dead."

It was what my own mother had told me when my father left us. I was ten. She had no other explanation. What else can you say to a child?

We drove off, headed west again. At least that time I'd managed to save a bit, and there was no stealing bread or gas.

Still, we ran out of cash about the same time we ran out of country, and we set ourselves up in Culver City, California. Neither of us had ever seen the ocean and we couldn't get enough of the tireless waves and the never-ending horizon. Not that we had much time to spend at the beach, what with finding a half-decent place to live and any kind of a job—although it turns out diners in California aren't much different from diners in Iowa, and my experience came in handy when I finally saw a help-wanted sign in a restaurant window on Wilshire Boulevard. But if I had a day off, I'd take Melissa out of school, and we'd coax the old Cutlass down to Venice, park on a side street right there by the pier. We'd sit on the sand all day long and watch the water and the seagulls and all those people, just like we belonged.

A year slipped by. One bright afternoon we were strolling back from the beach, arm in arm, singing a jingle we'd heard on the radio. The waves had been crashing on the shore, and the air tasted of the ocean, warm and salty.

"You look just like a movie star," I said, "with that tan and those dark glasses. May I have your autograph?"

She leaned into me and wrapped her arm around my waist, giggling. "Momma," she said, "can we come to the beach every day?"

"I wish we could, honey. I wish we could." I pulled the car keys out of my purse and was spinning them on my finger when the flashing red lights stopped me dead. Two patrol cars had the Cutlass blocked and a cop peered in the window, talking into a transmitter on his shoulder. I'd been so stupid! Of course Max would have reported what kind of car I was driving, and of course they'd been looking for it. We were plain lucky it hadn't been spotted up to then. A miracle.

I clamped my hand on Melissa's mouth, and we turned around. At the corner we slipped out of sight and ran up to Pacific Avenue. I still had the damn keys in my fist, but as we waited for a bus— Melissa pouting because I wouldn't tell her why the cops were looking in our car or why we'd run away like that—I pulled the car keys off the ring and dropped them in a trash can, heard the rustle of newspapers and Styrofoam as they sifted to the bottom. I don't know why, but that sound calmed me.

A close call like that teaches you to be careful: you can't outrun evil; you have to stay alert. So maybe it was a good thing, a lesson Melissa and I both needed to learn. But it seemed we definitely needed to get out of there, and just like that we were on the move again. I didn't even call the restaurant.

That time we took the Greyhound, since we didn't have a car anymore, and at least Melissa enjoyed the ride—something different, something she'd never done. I'd heard another waitress talk about her hometown, like she couldn't understand why she'd ever left and how much she wanted to get back there one day. It sounded like a nice place, so that's where we went. Winslow, Arizona.

That Doris woman comes out to the farmhouse porch. I know she won't see me, the Toyota's parked far enough away, but I duck down just the same. She holds her hand flat beyond the eaves, feeling the rain, and goes back inside. There's no sign of Max, but it's the middle of the day and I wonder if he's in the barn. Or if he's even alive. Until this minute, until the very second that I ask myself if he's in the barn, it never occurred to me Max might be dead, despite what I'd been telling Melissa for years, ever since we left Muscatine. He's older than me, had already been in the service and lived wild by the time we got together. Drank more than his share, at least until Melissa came along. God knows the years haven't been kind to any of us. What have I come all this way for, if the man isn't even here?

Right then, with the rain pouring down, Max comes out the barn door and breaks into a slow trot for the house. I've planned to just walk over and ring the bell, see the shock on his face that I'd have the nerve to show up. Or maybe he'd look past me to see if Melissa was standing there, or waiting in the car. I have my chance. He's inside, probably sitting down to lunch, tomato soup and half a bologna sandwich. But I can't do it; I'm not ready. I start the engine, sit there a bit longer staring blindly through the cracked windshield, and drive off.

Winslow reminded me of home, a small town, with shop-lined streets and slow-moving tourists. Except the shops sold turquoise jewelry and handicrafts. And it hardly ever rained. And the air smelled different, like hot, dried mud.

I was Julia there, still with the Iowa license, but no one cared who we were or where we came from. Starting in her new school, Melissa even agreed to use a different name. I let her choose, this time; Angelique is what she picked. Angelique. Where did the child come up with that? But I'd promised, soon she made friends, and the kids all called her Angel. She'd had a growth spurt by then and lost her baby fat, so the name seemed to fit. Used it with her myself most times, except when I was tired or anxious. Or angry.

I discovered you can make more money in a cocktail lounge than in a greasy spoon, although the customers are rowdier and the hours are rough. It got harder to keep an eye on Melissa, or know what she was up to half the time. At least it was too dark in that lounge for Tommy Carr or anyone else who might stumble in to recognize me. By then I'd done more than change my name. My hair used to be dull as clay, in a flip, had been that way since school and it never occurred to me to change, even when you didn't see anybody wearing that style anymore. But when we got to Winslow I went blond—trembling just to walk inside that beauty salon, it was such a big step—and while I was at it I had the girl do it up in a bouffant. Thought I'd choke from the hairspray, but I liked the way it turned out. So did Melissa. Said it made me look rich.

Whether it was the hair, or being around hard-drinking men every day, I got asked out fairly often. There was one guy, Timothy, a solid, tall soldier-type, down to the buzz cut and manners, who had me going for a while, whiskey breath and all. He'd hold doors for me, tell me my eyes twinkled in the moonlight, used his hands on me gently, the way men never do. He was married, though. He never said so, but I could tell. I asked him once, and after that he stopped coming around.

Then there was Paul: big rough hands, stained teeth, no mouth for small talk. I let him get away with hitting me once—a slap across my cheek that left a purple welt—but when it happened again I turned him loose. After Paul came Herb. Herb wore a purple polo shirt and blazer the first time I saw him, and kept patting his hair to make sure his comb-over was in place. I wanted to tell him he'd be more attractive, or at least less repulsive, if he just gave in to the baldness, but before I had a chance to do that he mentioned he was a doctor. A radiologist. But even radiologists can write prescriptions, and for one night we both got what we wanted.

When Samuel came into the lounge—I'd been there almost a year and a half—I noticed him first thing. He reminded me of Timothy, neat and well-groomed, except he was shy. He watched me ferry drinks from the bar for a long time but he didn't make a move, so I walked right up to his table, plopped down in the other chair, and introduced myself. He sat up straight, his eyes on fire.

"I'm a widower," he said, after we'd burned a couple of minutes on little things—the wildfires up North, the recent tourist invasion. "My wife committed suicide." It seemed an odd thing to tell someone he'd just met, but he was setting the ground rules. I understood that.

"I'm divorced," I said. I told him about moving to Winslow from Flagstaff, raising Angelique alone all those years, how Max—except I called him Jeffrey—how Jeffrey had abused us, Angel especially, and then went back East with a woman he'd met at work at the Westinghouse plant. And now we never saw him, and didn't even know for sure where he was, New Jersey we thought. The lies just spilled out of me, I couldn't stop, and I barely recognized myself by the time I finished. Sammy was close to tears.

I regretted it the next day, but I kept reminding myself that the ship had sailed, and if I wanted to hang on to good, gentle, sensitive Sammy, I could never go back and fix what I had done. On our first date, Sammy came by my apartment—a little two-bedroom in an adobe house that looked out on a brick courtyard and a cactus garden—with a stuffed bear for Angel. I pulled her into the kitchen, stranding Sammy at the front door.

"Remember," I whispered, right into her ear, "we've lived in Arizona forever, your Daddy moved back East somewhere, you don't even know where."

"But it's not true."

"Just do what I tell you, you hear?" I tried to keep my voice down but it got louder and louder, like a train coming fast. She was making me so angry, spoiling my chance with Sammy.

"But, Mommy—"

I smacked her good on the butt and pushed her into the living room, where Sammy sat rigid on our rented sofa.

"What do you say to Mr. Sam, sweetie?"

"Thank you," she mumbled, eyes on the bear, a cute little critter in a red-striped shirt and a sailor hat.

"Now run along, Angel," I said, watching Sammy.

He made it easy for me, rarely talked about the past, his or ours. Melissa did whatever she could to avoid him when he visited—coloring in her room, tea parties with all the stuffed animals she'd collected, half from Sammy, always trying to win her over.

Sammy took me out most nights I wasn't working, and Melissa usually stayed by herself. She said she didn't mind, so I didn't worry. It wasn't too long before he started sleeping over at our apartment on those nights. That first morning-after we were sitting in the kitchen, drinking coffee, giggling like naughty schoolkids. I heard Melissa's bedroom door open, her singing softly in the hall, slippers shuffling on the tile floor heading our way. When she saw Sammy, the sunny look on her face vanished.

"Say 'good morning' to Mr. Sam, Angel," I said.

Melissa scowled.

"I have to be going anyway," Sammy said, pushing up from the table.

"No. She has to learn manners." I grabbed Melissa's wrist and pulled her onto my lap. "Say it."

She lowered her head. I lifted her chin and squeezed both sides of her mouth until it made a pinched oval. "Say it!"

"Really, Julia, it's okay," Sammy said. He towered over us, weight shifting foot to foot.

"Say it!"

"Morning," Melissa managed, squirming off my lap. She ran out of the kitchen. Her bedroom door slammed.

It got better every time. Eventually, she'd let him cut her pancakes for her, and, once or twice, when he was there at her bedtime, she let him read her a story. Although I reminded her often to say we'd always lived in Arizona, in Flagstaff before we moved to Winslow, she still said next to nothing when he was in earshot.

For Melissa's twelfth birthday I planned a party. I wrote out invitations that she could give to her friends at school, little cards with a martini on the cover. I thought the theme was cute. I stole cocktail napkins from the lounge and set out pretzel sticks on the table, just like we did at work. I even put on my waitressing uniform—low-cut blouse, short black skirt, and black stockings— to serve the girls Shirley Temples. Sammy went to Baskin Robbins to pick up an ice-cream cake.

"My back is killing me," I said, swallowing a Darvon when the appointed hour had come and gone. Not a single little girl had shown up. When Melissa turned five, Max had organized a petting zoo with our own farm animals. He was the master of ceremonies in a three-ring circus, keeping the lambs in their pen, bottle-feeding a calf, producing baby chicks from a hat like the magician the kids all thought he was. Every child in the county must have been there; Melissa had talked about it for months.

"I hope your guests get here soon," Sammy said.

Melissa sat at the kitchen table twirling a drink umbrella. "No one's coming."

"They'll be here." Sammy peered out the front window and checked his watch. "They're just fashionably late."

"It was a dumb idea for a party," Melissa said, her voice thick. She ran to her room. The door slammed, a sound I'd become used to. When I followed and pushed the door open, expecting to see her sobbing into a pillow, I found her sitting on the floor, tearing the undelivered invitations into pieces.

On our six-month anniversary, Sammy took me to Red Lobster to celebrate. We had cocktails before dinner and then wine with the main course; he let me taste his scampi and I spooned nearly half my lobster Newburgh onto his plate—like an old married couple who shared everything. After the dishes were cleared away, the waiter left a small tray on the table with two mints and the check, and I went to the ladies room.

When I came back, Sammy was reaching into my purse. "I'm short of cash for the tip," he said, grinning. "Do you mind if I borrow a few dollars?" He had my wallet in his hand.

"No, of course—" I began, and held my breath. It wasn't quite a prayer, but I wished for him to grab the money and toss the wallet back. I closed my eyes, hoping that when I opened them he'd be standing to go, tucking the money under the plate.

But when I looked, Sammy's grin was gone and he was staring at the open wallet, my gritty driver's license picture squinting up at him just next to the great seal of the state of Iowa. Sammy blinked. He gazed at me, then back at the picture, then at me again.

"You never said anything about living in Iowa."

"It was a long time ago."

"2000, it says. Three years ago." His finger underlined the date of issue and lingered.

"No, no. That's a renewal. The original was ages back."

"Why an Iowa address? You said you moved here from Flagstaff."

"We were there such a short time. For Max's work. It wasn't worth mentioning."

"I thought your husband's name was Jeffrey."

"Yes, of course. Jeffrey. The other's a nickname. I don't think I like your tone, Sam. Stop questioning me. And please give that back." I held out my hand.

He riffed through the remaining bills, then the empty slots where Mona's credit cards had been. Thank God I'd had the sense to trash those. My mind raced to think what else there might be, maybe something with my real name on it. Mona was a cousin I could say, or—I grabbed for the wallet, but he yanked it out of my reach, knocking over a wine glass in the process. The grainy dregs bled into the tablecloth.

"Give me that," I said, too loudly. People were staring.

He slipped a finger under the license and removed it, along with a slip of paper. He unfolded it. "From Iowa," he said. "Three years ago. Pay stub. Your name."

"Sam," I said.

"I could overlook the pills, Julia. I could maybe even help you kick them. But this—"

"I can explain."

"Don't bother." Sammy dropped my wallet on the table, shook his head and backed away. I knew everyone in that restaurant was watching me, but I sat there a few minutes, used my napkin on my eyes as if I'd been crying, then got up, stood as tall as I could, and walked out.

The rain has stopped and there is patchy sun. The old house appears to glow for a moment and then, as a cloud passes over, dim. It's around time for supper and I've got Melissa in tow, dragged from the TV in our motel room where I've spent the afternoon dozing, doubting. Her eyes are stitched to a chirping Gameboy.

"Put that thing away," I say, and am ignored. She was so little when we left, and I've managed to confuse her over the years with stories of one-room shacks and notions of derelict trailers Max dragged us to, that she doesn't realize this is her own house, the house where she was born. Still, I thought she'd recognize the place.

"Now, please." I flip the mirror down and tease my hair, brush color onto my cheeks.

"Do I have to?"

After what we've been through together, I've told her, we're taking a much-needed vacation. We're visiting old friends, we lived in this town when she was a baby. She trails behind me, still watching the matchbook screen, kicks each step as we climb the porch, cracks gum in her mouth, glances sideways through the wisteria trellis, her eyes drawn to it, recalling the smell maybe or the long purple blooms. I knock on the door. I step out of the way, move Melissa forward, and steady my hands on her shoulders.

"Where are we?" she asks, her eyes finally bright with the bud of remembrance.

***

After Sammy, I swore off men, at least men who pretended they were in it for the long haul. I'd thought he was a sign we could stop running, that Melissa and I would finally have nice things, a nice place to live, a nice car, someone to treat us right. I thought he'd be good with Melissa. But when he walked out like that, I just didn't want to get my hopes up again.

"Probably two-timing us," I said to Melissa, tugging the earphones from her head so she'd hear me. "Probably has a family somewhere he didn't bother to tell us about."

She rolled her eyes. "You *lied* to him, Mom. You made *me* lie to him." How she'd grown. Almost a teenager, not too old for the dolls and stuffed animals, but experimenting with lipstick and eye shadow, the ponytail a memory, shutting me out with hip hop and boy bands. "Anyway, I'm glad he's gone."

"Time for us to move on, too, don't you think? Winslow's not right for me anymore." Too many old folks. Too many bills, too much back rent, too many fibs to keep straight.

"Whatever," she said, replacing the earphones, sinking back into the music.

If we were leaving Arizona, I thought it might be time to visit Momma, let her get reacquainted with her granddaughter. The last we'd talked on the phone, months and months before, she sounded weak, tired of it all.

"All that running's not good for Melissa," she'd said. "You should bring your girl home."

"We are home, Momma."

"What kind of home can *you* give her, Mona?" Her voice was low and raspy, halting.

So we bought a beat-up Toyota and headed east. Passing through Oklahoma, it occurred to me I ought to call Momma, hint that we'd be there in a few days, see what kind of response I got. The first time I phoned from the motel in Tulsa there was no answer, which seemed strange because I never thought Momma left the trailer much. The next time, just after Melissa had drifted off to sleep on our bed with the TV flickering at us, a man answered.

"Hello?" A tentative voice, sleep-blurred. I wasn't sure what to do. On TV, a getaway van careened around a corner, chased by two howling police cars.

"Hello," the man said again.

"Is Roberta there?"

"Who's this?" asked the man.

The question stole my breath. It didn't sound like Max, but was it someone Max had sent to find us? After such a long time, it didn't seem possible. Melissa stirred.

"Is that Mona?" he asked.

"Where's my mother?"

Dead. Months earlier. The man was Chet, an old flame who'd been living with her off and on and had stayed when she died. It had been so long since my last call. No one had known how to reach me.

With Momma gone there was no point going back, so we stayed right where we were. I didn't have to look far for work—the Best Western needed a desk clerk, and the manager, a cheerful black woman with dangly earrings, hired me on the spot. I enrolled Melissa in school—she'd dropped Angelique when we left Winslow and was now calling herself Tina, said it sounded more mature—and even found a nice little apartment. I had a steady stream of short-term boyfriends. She joined the Girl Scouts, then quit that. I needed more and more Darvon to manage the pain in my back; I knew Sammy'd been right about the pills but I couldn't quit on my own. Melissa had her first real date. I tried to be good with her, but it got harder and harder to keep track of things. And we went on that way for a couple of years, in Tulsa, Oklahoma.

One day about six weeks ago I came home from work early. I'd had trouble filling my prescription, so I could barely see from the pain in my back and the headache that usually went with it. I heard the awful music even before I had my key in the door, some punk band that Melissa worshipped, and once inside I recognized the sweet smell of marijuana.

I opened her door and the smoke blasted out as Melissa and an older, long-haired boy jumped from the bed and scrambled to cover themselves. The music screamed from Melissa's boom box. The boy struggled with his pants, and Melissa flapped her arms as if she could hide the cloud that hovered above her bed.

"You," I shouted over the band, pointing at the boy, "get the fuck out." I moved to the boom box, only succeeded in making it louder when I tried to shut it off, grabbed it with both hands, and heaved it against the far wall, where it exploded, littering the shag with shrapnel.

"Jesus," the boy said as he disappeared from the room. The door to the apartment slammed. The room seemed to spin, and I tasted vomit in my throat.

"How dare you barge in here," Melissa screamed. With the music silenced, her scream was deafening.

I lurched forward and grabbed her shoulders. "Don't you talk to me that way," I shouted, shaking her like a rag doll. "And you promised there'd be no drugs." I was pleading now, my head bursting. "And no sex, not yet."

"You're one to talk," she said through clenched teeth, pushing my hands away. "What about those sleazebags you bring home? You think I don't notice? You think I can't hear? And you can't even get out of bed without your fucking pills. You lie to get your pills. You'd steal if you had to. You'd—"

I slapped her, hard.

"I hate you!"

I slapped her again. And again. And again.

There stands stout Doris, peering out through the screen, wiping her hands on a checked terry dishcloth, consternation in her pinched eyes. And then recognition.

"Max," she calls over her shoulder, like a cough.

Max appears. He was a tall man—it was part of what attracted me when I was a girl—but now his neck droops forward, bringing his eyes almost level with mine.

"Yes?" he asks, his voice husky, old.

"Daddy?" asks Melissa, her shoulders tensing under my trembling hands. Is it the voice? Or the familiar smell? She steps back, confused—because to her he's dead—and surely remembering the picture I've painted of a monster.

"My Lord," says Max. He pushes the screen open.

"I . . . brought her back," I say. I know it's not that simple. He was never good at forgiving. He won't pretend it never happened. And for what I did, and what he's in for now—why should he?

Doris is there behind Max, her mouth open, staring. I wonder if she sees, somehow, why I've come back.

"Momma?" Melissa looks back at me, my little girl again, if just for a moment.

I nudge her toward Max, drop my hands from her shoulders. I think about running to the car, getting away before Max can do anything, heading back to Tulsa, or Winslow, or someplace new. But now, for the first time since I snatched Melissa from this very porch, I can't move.

WILLIAM & FREDERICK

The Armani shoes—the sleek indigo-black ones with the angel-hair laces he could never keep tied—were too big for William, but he slipped them on anyway. He'd wanted to wear one of Frederick's suits, too, maybe the newish Pierre Cardin that Frederick had liked because he swore the tiny black-and-white checks were slimming, the one William thought really made Frederick look like a circus clown, although love had kept him from saying so. But the suit was impossible on William, the shoulders drooping wide on both sides like little mutant fins, the sleeves dangling past his wrists, the flapping waist that suggested William might be a spokesman for Weight Watchers, except it wasn't *his* weight he'd lost. He couldn't wear that to the grand opening, but he didn't mind sliding around inside the Armanis, just for one day, and if it got too awful he had his clogs in the canvas tote. Surely no one would care if he made himself more comfortable inside his own store.

His own store. It had been Frederick's idea, the older man thoughtful as always, even with his guts turning to jelly and a daily joint the only thing that had still worked to keep the pain at bay. "Look, sweetie," he'd said as William helped him into the tub one night near the end, "this is perfect. It'll keep you busy, put food on the table, which God knows you need, you skinny little thing, and it's all I've got to give you." William had been unable to speak. "And you can stay here," Frederick had added, with a weak little wave that scattered rose-scented bubbles across the black-and-white tiles, "at least until Cassie gets wind of it." Then he nearly sank under the water until William got him propped up and started scrubbing his back with the loofa. Cassie. William hadn't met her, and Frederick usually referred to her as the evil stepsister, the reason Frederick hadn't inherited the house from his aunt outright.

And it was Frederick who'd found the empty retail space and negotiated the lease and hired a couple of his former students, tobacco-chewing dropouts, to move the stuff in, although it was just as well he hadn't been around to see the brutes manhandle even the most delicate pieces.

As William scuffed down Central Avenue, braced against a chilly November wind and stopping every so often to tie the shoes, he could scarcely believe that at the tender age of twenty-three he was on his way to the shop that he owned, the shop to which only he had the key, the ancient black safe of which only he could unlock, and that in just a few minutes after opening the door of his shop, no more than that surely, he would be pressing all the buttons on the complicated new cash register Frederick had ordered just for him, to ring up the first of many glorious sales. His own store.

William & Frederick. That had been William's idea, and it pleased him. They'd wanted to call the store Blue Ridge Antiques, but when Frederick checked around, thumbing through the phone book, a blustery call to directory assistance, an Internet search for listings up and down the Valley, he turned up no fewer than fifty shops with that name, including one hidden away inside the ghastly mall outside town, and another a few miles south, that looked, when William drove Frederick's Riviera down to investigate, as though it had been somebody's garage, converted into a flea market, half an acre of rickety tables covered with muddy tarps, and a hand-lettered sign out front that said, "Make an Offer! Swap Meet Saturday." But the perfect name had come to William two weeks ago while he sipped a *latte* in Java Mountain, watching the lanky kid behind the counter flirt with the fuchsia-haired Madonna, worried about the letter he'd received that morning, just gibberish to him, from the lawyers handling the estate, the Richmond firm of Botts & Allen, whose offices had impressed William with their dignified style, plush Persians and early Americana. That's it, William said to himself, or maybe out loud because the girl with the freakish hair turned to look. An elegant, refined name, to sell elegant, refined antiques. William & Frederick.

It wasn't all elegant stuff, though, William had to admit. Frederick had owned some fabulous pieces, collected over half a century of shopping and travel, and roomfuls he'd inherited from the aunt he'd claimed was royalty. "We're all queens here, honey," William had said, mortified when Frederick didn't laugh. "Well, she *was*," he'd insisted, running his hand over the dark surface of the walnut Queen Anne highboy, the gem of the collection. Then there was the mahogany breakfast table that had its own name. Duncan Phyfe, Frederick called it, as if it were a guest in the house and not a piece of furniture. "Let's join Duncan Phyfe in the kitchen," he'd say, determined that they should actually use the thing, despite William's fear of damaging a valuable antique. "What," Frederick had said, "you don't think the colonists ever spilled their tea?" The one piece that really unnerved William was the Khmer bust of Buddha, which Frederick said he'd acquired for a blowjob in Bangkok in the sixties. William didn't doubt the price, a currency familiar to him, but Bangkok didn't sound like the kind of place Frederick would have been caught dead in—dusty and smelly and filled with women on the make. That wasn't Frederick at all. When he'd arranged everything in the shop before the grand opening, William had settled the bust into a corner and, when its stony eyes followed him everywhere as he dusted and shifted and rearranged, hoping customers wouldn't notice the little nicks and scratches that cropped up everywhere like acne from his not-so-long-ago adolescence, he draped over it a soiled batik sarong from that same Asian trip. But in addition to those valuable artifacts, William had elected to display stuff that people in their god-forsaken, drought-parched village might actually buy: Frederick's childhood rocking horse; a pair of glass candlesticks, with red wax cascading down the sides from last Christmas; five shelves of dusty books, "The Classics" Frederick had called them when he'd tried to get William to read something other than mysteries and true crime, and there were plenty more where they came from in the den at home; a yellow porcelain teapot that William had no use for now that he could drop the pretense that the love of chamomile was something he shared with Frederick, even though he knew Frederick knew it was a sham and that William had devised the ruse solely for his benefit. Thank God he could drink coffee again.

William stopped just short of his store, in the glare of the tacky gift shop Frederick had always refused to step foot in, but that William admired for its clever inventory, like those darling salt and pepper shakers in the shape of Dalmatians. He gazed at his future. His store wasn't on high-traffic Main Street—the rent for both vacant spots there had been too expensive, one next to the coffee house and one tucked between the tavern and the town's only nail salon—but he could see his door from the corner of Central and Main, a location Frederick had been sure would guarantee success. Of course, the door was below street level, five steps down into a tiny courtyard—more like an overgrown window-well that collected leaves and cigarette butts and any other trash that blew down the hill from the courthouse, and would probably fill up with grimy snow come winter—but the gold lettering on the window, William & Frederick, was visible, even from across the street. It sparkled a little, William thought. He stooped to tie his shoelace.

Dodging a red pickup and then a Ford van with a crater on the passenger side that looked like the kind of dent an old cannonball would make, although William couldn't imagine how that had happened, maybe some Civil War reenactment gone awry, he crossed the street in midblock. He didn't have to fish in his pocket for the key because he was wearing it around his neck on one of those lanyards, a gift from Frederick because William, who had never owned anything valuable to speak of, had a knack for losing keys. It didn't matter so much, really, because the house was never locked—most folks didn't bother unless they lived on the west side of town—and Frederick hadn't let William drive the Buick except on special occasions. So the house key, the one key William had possessed until the shop came along, was more a token of Frederick's affection than it was of any practical use.

William didn't bother to take the lanyard off, just bent over and fit the key in the lock, and jiggled it a little like the real estate agent—that handsome, thick-haired Mr. Lynch who had seemed to hurry through their appointments—had demonstrated when he showed them the property. A musty smell greeted William (why hadn't he ever noticed it when all this stuff was cluttering up the house?), and new paint, the lilac they'd picked over the bleeding-heart pink because the pink was too passionate, Frederick's color, and was sure to bring up all kinds of memories he didn't want to deal with. The lilac was just right, soothing and soft, a color that made you think of your grandmother's garden, which was exactly what customers in an antique shop should think. Or at least that's what Frederick had asserted when he told William the rest of his plans for the store.

"I don't want you going back there," Frederick had said, and William knew he meant back where they'd met, as if William could ever think of hustling again. Frederick had rescued him, given him things, *taught* him things. Now he knew about wine and music and antiques. A little, anyway. That other life was over.

"No," William said. "I'd rather kill myself. But at least that way we would be together." That was something else they talked about, how fate had united them when Frederick popped into a gay bar in D.C. and found William, and nothing like a little colon cancer was going to tear them apart, at least not for long. Frederick wouldn't listen to that, though.

He shook his head. "You'll meet someone, honey. You'll move on. I know that. But in the meantime, there's enough stuff in this old house to keep an antique store going a long time, and when it's gone you can buy some junk and sell that. It's decided, then." And William had gone along to keep Frederick happy. The momentum had been too strong to fight. "A shop. You know, I've always wanted to run a shop, keep the customer happy, service is our business and all that. Where everyone expects you to be gay anyway, so it's no surprise when it turns out you are. And I'd paint it lilac, like my grandmother's garden."

Lights on. William hadn't realized before just how dark the space was, on an overcast fall morning, on this side street with no direct light anyway and the shop window half-hidden by the stairs. Even with the fluorescents the place felt like a cave, or the bowels of a ship, and William made a mental note to use the proceeds of his first sale to install better lighting, maybe a couple of torchieres like Frederick had shown him in one of his magazines, or a spotlight aimed at that nasty Buddha. Maybe it would even help sell the thing. He took a quick look around, sure he wouldn't get another chance once the store flooded with customers, a last-minute inventory of Frederick's life before the hordes started picking at the brocade on the Venetian divan, testing the strength of the spindly comb-back Windsor chair—the one Frederick had never let anyone sit in, not even featherweight William, for fear it would collapse into splinters—or caressing the seductive satin of the Rococo rosewood chairs, the pair that Frederick had been given by a friend, about whom he never said any more, no matter how much William pleaded or forgave him for past indiscretions.

William wanted just one last minute of respite before he started haggling with the gaggle of bargain hunters: "It's not quite what I'm looking for, and isn't that a burn mark on the top, and I saw the exact same piece at Blue Ridge Antiques for a third what you're asking, and I couldn't possibly go any higher than . . ." William's eyes landed on a Georgian wing chair that had been one of Frederick's favorites at home, angled by the fireplace, perfect for a quiet evening with a book and that awful cognac he liked, while William curled up on the couch with a Heineken. The leather was caramel, and spidery veins had emerged on the seat where it sagged into a bowl.

"Come sit with me for a second, honey," said the chair, although it was Frederick's lilt that William heard.

William turned around, slowly, making sure he was as alone in the store as he thought he was. "I am not getting into a conversation with this chair," he said. "I'm not. Do you hear me, Freddy?" He spun on his heel and saw the Buddha, hiding under the sarong. "Do you hear me? So please just shut up." William knew perfectly well that the furniture wasn't talking, any more than the cozy tub at home called to him, or the big four-poster in their bedroom whispered in his ear. He wasn't crazy. He missed Frederick, that's all. He missed candlelight suppers of exotic dishes he'd never heard of before, he missed that awful opera screeching from the stereo, he missed being corrected whenever he mispronounced a word. He missed Frederick.

He hopped to the cash register, always reluctant to step on the grizzled Heriz rug from the living room, even though Frederick had insisted rugs were meant to be walked on. "They're not fragile, honey," he'd said more than once. "Some camel probably fornicated on this rug." William had been unconvinced. "All the more reason not to walk on it," he always said. William took up his position behind the counter, turned on the cash register, saw by Frederick's marble-and-gold Belgian mantel clock that it was almost ten, and eyed the door, ready for business.

Just before noon, William still stood behind the counter. The door had yet to open, although he had watched countless legs go by, legs cloaked in jeans and cowboy boots, bony legs in running shorts and Nikes, elephantine legs that ended in what looked to be fuzzy slippers, shapely legs in high heels behind a stroller. A little girl peeked out of the carriage and waved at William. William waved back.

"Well, it's understandable that business would be slow the first day," William said aloud. "I'm sure there'll be a crowd at lunch."

"I'm sure you're right," said the wing chair.

"I'm not talking to you," shouted William.

When no one came in during lunch, William looked for ways to keep busy. He took down the grand opening sign he'd taped to the window, got out the Windex to attack a streak he'd noticed, and put the sign back up. He took Frederick's collection of Toby jugs out of the glass case under the cash register and dusted each one, wiped the shelves, and put the jugs back, careful to leave them facing forward, as Frederick had shown him after dusting them at home. Then William pulled the books off the shelves and set about arranging them, in alphabetical order by author, and wondered if maybe he should kill some time by reading one of them.

"Frederick would be pleased," he said.

"And astonished," said the bookshelf, a handsome oak lawyer's cabinet with glass doors and white porcelain knobs. "But what you really ought to do is move a chair outside, so people can see some signs of life."

William backed away. "Shut up!" But when he thought about it he saw it wasn't a bad idea, and he settled on one of the sturdier pieces, a heavy Roycroft chair from the dining set Frederick had been so proud of because he'd assembled it from different arts and crafts designers—the Greene Brothers, Gustav Stickley, even Frank Lloyd Wright. William lugged the thing out to the sidewalk.

"Ouch," said the chair, when William bumped it into the door. "Be careful."

"Sorry," said William. He went back inside, hopped over the rug, and grabbed a book off the shelf without looking to see what it was, then sat outside, with his knees together as Frederick had taught him, Frederick's gray cashmere sweater over his shoulders, waiting to be noticed. The street was empty. William opened the book and read: "Call me Ishmael."

At three, William was hungry. He made another mental note, this time to bring his lunch in the future, but on opening day he'd been so sure he wouldn't have time to eat anyway, he hadn't bothered to pack anything. And he was reluctant to close, even for a minute, to run down to Java Mountain for coffee and a bagel, because surely in the time it took to get there, have that slow-witted boy with the snake tattoo on his wrist, cute as he was, make the sandwich and the *latte*, someone would have come looking to buy the highboy and gone away disappointed. He stood up, sleepy from reading about the doomed whaling voyage, and took a step toward the shop door, then stepped back, worried even now that he'd miss a customer if he took a break. His stomach growled.

"Put a note on the door, sweetie," said the chair. "I'll be right here, and people can wait."

"I suppose you're right," said William. He scribbled a little sign—Back in 5—and taped it to the door. He ran up to the corner, took a right on Main, and ran back, slipping inside the Armanis both ways, confident there'd be someone in the chair when he returned.

"Did anyone come?" William asked the chair, wheezing from the unfamiliar exertion.

"Nope," said the chair. "Nobody. Nada. Zippo. Zero. Zilch."

"Shut up," screamed William, and looked around sheepishly when he remembered he was standing on the sidewalk. He sat down, sipped the *latte* and nibbled at his bagel, toasted, with rosemary chicken salad, no tomato, and opened the book again, this time in the middle to see if the action might have picked up by then. "Chapter 49. The Hyena." Hyena? What happened to the damn whale? "There are certain queer times and occasions in this strange mixed affair we call life when a man takes this whole universe for a vast practical joke . . ."

"You got that right," William said, and closed the book. He dragged the dining chair inside.

At five, William banged the "enter" button on the cash register, heard the satisfying bing-bong when the drawer popped open, and counted the day's receipts. Zero, of course. "Nada, zilch," said the chair. He certainly didn't remember selling anything, but he considered the possibility, likelihood even, that he had spaced out, suffered temporary amnesia perhaps, because surely there had been a steady stream of customers, it being opening day for the elegant new antique shop near the corner of Central and Main, a location that couldn't miss, painted in surefire lilac, William & Frederick, a welcome addition to commerce in the sleepy hamlet. He closed the drawer.

"Good night," said the chair.

"Good night," said William.

Although the first day had been disheartening, even frightening because it raised the specter of poverty that his life with Frederick had, until now, allowed him to nearly forget, William arrived the next morning armed with a rosy outlook. For one thing, the shop was less lonely than the house. He'd moved so many of Frederick's things into the cramped store, and they'd been so vocal while the hours dragged on, that he actually looked forward to leaving the echo chamber that had once been the living room of the Victorian mansion and having a chat with the wing chair. Even if no customers appeared, at least he'd have someone to talk to. Maybe the Louis XVI armoire would speak up today. William had always wanted to learn French.

By the end of the first week, though, William was truly discouraged, the talkative antiques being little relief in the end, a steady cinema of bleak alternatives playing in his head—getting a real job, seeking out the brother he knew he had somewhere but hadn't spoken to in a decade, going back to the bar in D.C. where he'd first latched onto Frederick, almost as hungry and desperate now as he had been then. The furniture tried to cheer him up, assuring him it was only a matter of time, that the breakthrough would come, that he only needed to be patient. William listened, dusted everything as lovingly as he had seen Frederick do it, and even tried to read more about the devilish whale. At home he'd painted a new sign to hang in the window, "Grand Opening Sale," but it hadn't enticed a single browser into the store, much less a paying customer, and since it blocked what little natural light he had, William took it down.

On Saturday morning, he opened the glass case to take out the Toby jugs yet again, to remove for the fifth straight day dust that hadn't had a chance to settle from the first cleaning, when the shop door scraped open.

"Helloooo," crooned the woman who entered, a behemoth in a flowered dress, with overflowing chest and hips, breathless from the five steps down. She looked vaguely familiar to William, as half the town did. Whenever he and Frederick had ventured out of the house, resolved to ignore pointing fingers and stage whispers, Frederick offered William a running commentary on the townsfolk. "That's Bobby Cabe, a drunken old backwoodsman who tried to pick a fight with me once because he thought I was staring at him, not that I'd be the least bit interested in him even if he were the last fag on earth. Now he's just belligerent and babbles on about fairies, and it's not me he's talking about, I'm reasonably sure. That one over there is Mildred Rutledge, from the high school. From what I hear, she's fond of young boys, so you better look out. And that one, the one with the white hair bent over double like she's looking for a dime, that's Henrietta Doak. She's ninety years old and still drives herself around in her late husband's Cadillac, so when you see her coming, best get out of the way." William wasn't sure if this woman was one Frederick had described, but he wouldn't have been able to remember anyway, despite her eye-popping girth, caught up as he was in the excitement of having his first customer.

In his haste, he dropped the smallest Toby jug on the glass shelf and gasped when the handle, a delicate, gray thing in the shape of a dolphin, or a whale maybe, or at any rate some big fish, rolled away, sheared clean from the face that made up the body of the jug, apparently a seafarer of some sort, William couldn't tell. A mental note to glue the fish back on, and William donned his widest smile, stuck out his hand as Frederick had suggested even with the most unlikely buyers—although this woman looked as likely as William could imagine—and welcomed the giantess into the shop. Mrs. Benson, as it turned out.

"I knew Frederick," she said in a low, sympathetic voice, as if they were at the funeral, although that had been over a month ago, early October, and no one from town had been there except the lesbian couple who ran a candle and macramé shop out on Sparksburg Pike plus a handful of Frederick's former students. "He might not have known me, though," she admitted. "My boy Joshua was in his literature class for a while, but we put a stop to that when we heard." Heard what, William wanted to ask, but even around Frederick, gentle, patient Frederick, he'd been afraid to ask questions because it seemed like the answer was always something he was supposed to have known in the first place but, he usually rationalized, he'd been too busy just surviving to learn. His confusion must have been scrawled on his face, because Mrs. Benson whispered, in a pitying voice that said, as clearly as if the words had come out of that cavernous mouth, "don't tell me you didn't know," along with the words she actually spoke: "About his illness."

Oh, that. He had cancer, it wasn't the other, William longed to say, looked over at the wing chair, the most outspoken of the collection, and shook his head, silently apologizing.

"Is there something in particular you're looking for, Mrs. Benson?" That's what Frederick had told him to say, wasn't it? Get the customer to commit to a quest, put the Holy Grail in her hands, and you've made the sale. Assuming you had the Holy Grail in stock, of course, and hadn't offered the Golden Fleece instead.

"Just browsing," she said.

William took up his post behind the cash register while Mrs. Benson pawed over Frederick's Waterford goblets, and the silver cake server that William really should have taken to a jeweler to appraise, but that seemed too crass somehow, and an insult to Frederick. Mrs. Benson stumbled into the Victorian writing table— a one-of-a-kind mahogany jewel on which Frederick had written his letters and lists, recorded every household expenditure, even graded remedial compositions—and she looked over at William with stiletto eyes (so disturbing in a woman that large) as though he most certainly had put the table in that spot for the sole purpose of injuring her. William shrugged, hoping it conveyed his meaning, which was, I'm terribly sorry, but I hope in your oafishness you haven't damaged Frederick's desk, lady, or there'll be hell to pay.

Mrs. Benson browsed awhile longer, and picked up and carried around with her as if it were a watermelon, a pear-shaped coppery vase that Frederick had said was Ming but to William just looked Chinese. William hadn't wanted to know *what* Frederick had done to acquire that piece, and couldn't bear to watch what this horrible woman was doing to it now. She sat for a minute in the wing chair that William could hear groaning under her incredible bulk, ran her fingertips over the cracked leather, then struggled up and over to the bookshelves, and lifted her glasses to read the titles. She even took one out to thumb the pages. But her wandering eyes always came back to the offending writing table.

"How much is it?" Mrs. Benson's voice had lost both its ingratiating melody and funereal whisper, and she was now all business. "Your best price, of course."

This was the moment Frederick had tried to prepare him for, the first negotiation with a customer. There was so much to consider! He wanted to make his first sale, of course, because he had to admit that things were not going well and he'd been so sure the money would just be rolling in at this point, and there was always the apparition of the evil stepsister lurking in his subconscious, so a sale would be a good thing, an omen of better things to come. But he couldn't start out too low, could he, because the desk had some value, and not only the price Frederick had paid for it or the services performed in Paris or New York or wherever, but it had belonged to Frederick! Frederick used it! Frederick treasured it! On the other hand, there was the rent, and if he didn't sell this piece and several more by the end of the month, William would have to dip into the cookie jar of cash Frederick had filled for him, and as Frederick had explained over and over again, that was not—what was the word Frederick had used?—sustainable.

But, despite all the planning, Frederick hadn't gotten around to telling William what the prices should be for anything. What did William know? He'd never sold a thing, apart from his own companionship, unless you could count that fiasco behind the men's fragrance counter at Macy's one of his regulars had finagled for him, and William had walked away from that job during a coffee break. Too stressful, too much to remember. Frederick had begun to talk about antique prices once, but somehow the subject of his stepsister had intruded and he'd become so upset, so overcome with what it would mean to William when she eventually showed up to claim the house and whatever William hadn't managed to sell by then, that he'd been unable to continue. He had gone downhill fast after that, barely able to speak, too weak to leave the house, too horrified by his appearance to allow visitors. And now William was on his own.

He opened a notebook, a black three-ring binder, and looked for the writing table on the list. Frederick had made the list years ago for insurance purposes, and when they were going through his papers, near the end, he had discovered it and handed it to William. "Perfect," he'd said, in a breathless gasp. "An inventory. Just what you need, my boy." And William had put the list in the binder, a dusty torn thing he'd found in the attic, and had decided that the values assigned for insurance purposes surely were the least he should try to get for each item. Hadn't Frederick called it perfect? He ran his finger down the page to the writing table, then across the row to the value, and closed the book. But wait, he thought, that's where I should end up, so I'll add a little for bargaining purposes, and then I'll give her a discount and we'll all be happy.

"Because you are such a delightful woman, I could let you have this darling table for . . ." William began, imitating as best he could the warble Frederick had demonstrated repeatedly, and remembering what Frederick had said about flattering both the customer and the purchase, to make them think they were made for each other, ". . . five thousand dollars." The woman's jaw dropped. Comically, William thought. He wondered what he'd done wrong.

"You're joking, of course," she said, laughing.

Was the price absurdly low? It seemed expensive to William, but then he'd never lived in the world of objects until he'd met Frederick. For years, after running away from his mother and stepfather's home in New Jersey, his older brother already free, off in the Army, the only thing on his mind had been food and shelter, and sometimes getting high, and after a while even food and shelter receded in importance. But then Frederick had rescued him and brought him home to the country and the house filled with curio cabinets, lace tablecloths, real china plates, engraved silverware. Frederick had tried to teach him, but there was only so much a boy could absorb.

How could he know the real value? Too low? Or was the price too high? That must be it, William realized. Frederick wouldn't have put a low value on the insurance forms, even William understood that, when he stopped to think about it. He might have inflated the value a tiny bit, right?

"I could consider a discount," William said, reciting the dialogue he'd learned from his lover, his mentor and savior. "One shouldn't really bargain with the customer," Frederick had insisted. "Bargaining is so . . . tacky. But one may offer a discount. A special price. A once-in-a-lifetime opportunity."

"I bet you could," said the leviathan, and ran her bloated finger over the table one more time. "I'll give you fifty bucks for it. And that's because I hit the jackpot at bingo last night." She pulled a wad of bills from her purse and counted out two twenties and ten wrinkled ones. William hesitated, felt Frederick pushing him to take it, heard the armoire whispering that rent day was just around the corner, actually lifted his hand to touch the cash, when out of the corner of his eye he saw the Buddha, shaking his head under the sarong. William put his hand in his pocket.

"No," he said, taking a step back from the counter. "It's worth much more than that."

"I see," said Mrs. Benson. "Bingo has its limits, I'm afraid." She stuffed the bills back in her purse and moved to the door, turned the knob, pulled it open, raised her foot to step out.

"Wait," said William.

Mrs. Benson closed the door and grinned. Maliciously, William thought. She reached into her purse and waved the cash at him.

He looked at the floor. "No," he said. "I can't."

The following week, William's expectations were lower. He'd put the Armanis away in Frederick's cedar closet, along with the checked suit, the cashmere sweater and all the rest of his clothes. He'd have to give them away or, better yet, leave them for Cassie to deal with. William's Dockers, that Frederick had bought him when he couldn't stand to see him in jeans any longer, and the clogs—Frederick bought those, too, of course—would do just fine. It's not as if anyone would see him anyway, tucked away in the dark basement. He arrived at the shop just at ten, a lunch packed, nothing fancy, a bruised apple and expired yogurt, no reason to think that the situation had changed, especially now that his one and only customer, the enormous Mrs. Benson, would spread the word that his shop was too expensive and that he, skinny, pasty little William, would never make it in the world without Frederick. On the way, he'd stopped at the Ace Hardware and picked up some glue, the only kind he knew, the milky white stuff that smelled like pudding, tasted a bit like it, too, if he remembered right, and set about fixing the little Toby jug. That done, he pulled the book off the shelf and settled into the wing chair. If I'm going to be bored to death, not to mention starving and poor, he thought, I might as well do what Frederick was after me all the time to do. "Call me Ishmael. Some years ago—never mind how long ago, having little or no money in my purse—"

The shop door swung open and a gust turned the page.

"Hellooo. Anybody home?"

It was that colossus again, this time with a woman who could have been her twin in tow, or rather her shadow, William thought, since she looked to be just a deli slice compared to the big woman's beefy slab. And anyway, their resemblance might only have been an illusion, as William realized he might have lived his whole life so far thinking that all old women looked exactly the same, only in different dimensions, with the salon-curled, blue-gray helmet and the high-collared, flowered dress and gold broach.

"This is Lydia, and I told her all about how charming you were and how you had some wonderful goodies in your shop and those candlesticks would look just fabulous on her mantel and how much do you want for them?" Mrs. Benson tugged Lydia to the armoire, where the candlesticks sat in semi-darkness. William had struggled out of the chair while she spoke and now opened his binder with the insurance list. He ran his finger down the page, but didn't see the candlesticks anywhere, which was no surprise because at home he'd found them under the sink in the powder room and knew they'd either been forgotten, or worthless. He picked one up and then the other, pleased with their heft, and even the dripped wax cheered his fingers, reminding him of his last Christmas with Frederick. He set them down gently on the counter and looked again in the binder. He ran his finger down the page one more time and stopped when he came to the armoire, value $15,000.

"I can let you have the pair for, let's see," William said, stalling, hoping they'd think he was calculating a discount off the asking price, when in fact he had no idea what number would be high enough to keep this gargantuan and her shadowy friend from buying the candlesticks, "I think, maybe, I suppose, two hundred dollars."

The wraith called Lydia opened her purse and pulled out a checkbook, but Mrs. Benson laughed so loudly the Buddha's sarong fluttered, and Frederick's rocking horse launched into motion. Mrs. Benson shook her head and laid a meaty hand on her friend's arm. Lydia looked up at her, obviously puzzled.

"You're a silly boy, William. No doubt this appealed to dear, sweet Frederick." She raised her eyebrows, and William understood she wasn't talking about Frederick's weakness for antiques. "But it's no way to run a business." With that, Mrs. Benson pulled Lydia, whose hand still clutched her checkbook and a fountain pen, up the stairs. The window shuddered, William thought, when the door slammed behind them.

"Now you've done it," said the highboy. "You had the fish on the line and let it get away."

"But at least the store is still afloat," said the wing chair. "For now."

"Forget the list, *mon cher*," said the armoire. "Go low."

In the afternoon, a young couple came in, a sloppy bra-less teenager with a pierced eyebrow, and a slim young man about William's age in khakis and a polo shirt, a silver ring on his thumb. William watched his careful steps, trailing the heedless girl. They looked at everything, laughing and poking at each other, "you're such a nerd," said the girl, and "at least I don't have a tattoo on my butt," said the young man. She called him Donnie, he called her Pammy, more like sister and brother than a couple.

"Is there something I can help you with?" he asked them.

"We were just looking," said the girl, pawing through a drawer full of costume jewelry. William didn't want to think about why Frederick had a drawer full of costume jewelry.

"Yeah, just looking," said the man, now keeping his eyes on William, straightening his collar. He stuck his hand out, thin and pasty, a light grip, like William's own. "I'm Donnie." Now the girl turned around to look, eyes wide.

"William," said William.

The girl clucked, grabbed Donnie and pulled him out the door. Donnie waved.

At home that night, there was mail. Addressed to him. He never got mail, but enjoyed the ritual of opening the box and going through the catalogs and advertisements and charity solicitations still being delivered for Frederick. This was a pale-blue envelope, the kind you might expect to be scented, with his name on it, a return address in California, and a regular first-class stamp, not one of those telltale bulk postage stamps he'd noticed on all his other mail. Frederick's mail. Who did he know in California?

It was from Cassie, the wicked stepsister. She'd just heard, was deeply saddened, sorry she and Frederick hadn't been closer, and by the way she'd be arriving next week to turn the house over to a realtor she'd hired, and would William be so kind as to be gone by the time she got there? William sank to the window seat, clutching the letter, pictured Frederick in his silk robe descending the stairs, Frederick reading by the fire, Frederick beating eggs for a soufflé.

What to do?

The next morning was damp and drizzly and William was happy to open the shop, shake out his umbrella, and ease into the wing chair to wait and think. There was still room in the shop, he saw, especially if he started piling things up, so he could call those awful boys Frederick had hired and ask them to bring another load over from the house. William didn't have much of his own to move, he could use one of Frederick's suitcases and still have room for some more of Frederick's things, and until something turned up he could sleep on the divan, shower at the Y maybe, and things would be fine. "You'll see," he said to the armoire. There was no answer.

He was still sitting there, gazing out the window, when he saw a pair of skinny legs in tight black jeans go by. Then the same legs went by in the other direction, stopped and crouched down, and that guy from the other day, Donnie, was looking in, upside down, grinning, William thought, but it was hard to tell that way, with the chin at the top. Donnie waved, and then his face popped out of sight and the legs skipped away. William felt a chill.

The titan came back, with Lydia in tow. "You silly boy," Mrs. Benson said, opened her purse and pulled out the bills she'd offered before. Lydia peeked around her megalithic friend and flashed her checkbook at William, a narrow grin on her lips.

"Forget your pride, *mon petite chou*," whispered the armoire. "Take the money," said the wing chair, "what choice do we have?" "Cassie is coming," said the highboy. William backed into the counter, rattling the Toby jugs on the glass shelves, and nodded as the whale closed in.

He slid out of her path, spun around to the cash register and pressed the buttons. Nothing happened. He looked up at her and shrugged. Pressing harder on the numbers, he hit "enter" with the heel of his hand, as if he just hadn't been convincing enough the first time, as if the machine would not allow him to surrender Frederick to this goliath. Out of the corner of his eye he saw Donnie's legs again, the black jeans, moving slowly now, stopping just at the steps. With a sheepish grin toward Mrs. Benson, William felt around the back of the box and threw the switch, felt the hum of power in his fingers, and rang up the sale, the insurance list forgotten. The drawer popped open and William slipped the bills inside, while Lydia wrote out her check—twenty dollars, Mrs. Benson had decreed—for the candlesticks.

"I'll pull the Lincoln around in a few minutes," said Mrs. Benson, breezing out, with Lydia in her wake. While the door was still open, Donnie stepped in.

William pretended to busy himself at the cash register, which for the first time actually harbored cash, but watched Donnie move through the store, examining everything he and the girl had seen already, making his way deeper inside, stopping again at the pile of costume jewelry. He turned toward William with a tiara in his hand, slipped it into his wispy blonde hair and blushed crimson, then set it down on the counter. "How much is it?"

"A dollar?" guessed William, suppressing a laugh. Donnie's fingers brushed William's palm when he handed him the bill, and they both turned away. William felt himself blushing now, too.

He'd barely finished the small sale when the door whooshed open again. A young couple—newlyweds from Philadelphia, they announced right away, as if that somehow was going to make a difference in any price he might quote them and, William had to admit, it did incline him toward a bigger number than he would have otherwise—instantly moved in opposite directions, the woman asking William about the highboy, then the armoire, while the husband shouted questions from the back about a dusty school desk he'd noticed in the corner. "It's from the oldest school in the county, a real collector's item," William lied loudly to the husband, with a wink to Donnie. "Previously owned by royalty," he crowed to the wife. The door opened again and an elderly couple came in and started nosing around, and they were all still in the store when Randy from Java Mountain strolled in, waved at William, and began fingering the books. Donnie leaned against the counter. William pretended not to notice.

As William was writing up the chair for the young couple, watching how the dark finger hair curled over the man's wedding ring while he steadied the checkbook, the older couple asked for the price of the armoire and this time William halved the insurance estimate, told them there was room for discussion and let them mull it over, and in the meantime Randy had grabbed a couple of books off the shelf and stood at the register with his wallet open.

Donnie still leaned. Oh my, thought William, this is just as I'd imagined it would be. The world isn't going to come crashing down after all! Let Cassie come!

Randy had gone with his books and the old couple was still examining the armoire. William would be sorry to see it go, but selling the most expensive piece in the store would be a real coup, even at the more realistic price, and he left them alone to talk themselves into it.

Mrs. Benson's Lincoln pulled up out front, idled there, a little cotton candy cloud of exhaust out the back, and he knew it was finally time. He leaned over the writing desk, tried to hold both ends and lift, but the table dragged its feet. William laughed at himself. You are a silly boy, aren't you, he thought, the table doesn't have feet. Well, it does, but . . . He leaned over again and it still seemed as though the table was reluctant, but William knew perfectly well what was happening. He wasn't a total dunce, despite what his stepfather might have thought. It wasn't the furniture who was foot-dragging. Donnie hopped around the counter, touched his hand to William's shoulder, grabbed the other side of the table, and together they lifted.

WHITE SWANS

I.

Elton Hoffman peered out the hotel window at the jumble of signs and billboards, searching for anything familiar among those indecipherable Chinese symbols. On the long flight over—the interminable, expectant flight on which sleep was impossible—he had read about them, trying to absorb what he could of the culture and language, but it was still beyond him how the locals could make sense of the swirls and squiggles, as random-looking as hen scratches. Elton shook his head and tried to shut out Lucinda's exhausted sobs.

Not just Lucinda's. Counting the baby, there were two females bawling in their cramped quarters, sparring with the piped-in Christmas carols, and Elton wasn't sure how much more he could take. Lucinda wiped away her tears with the coarse Chinese tissue she'd already complained about, and then, as if the newness of it all didn't frighten her one bit, as if mothering came naturally to her even without giving birth, she reached into the rickety crib, picked up nine-month-old Megan, and kissed the baby's cheek, rough and red as a shop-rag. Mother and daughter whimpered together. Elton wanted a cigarette.

Lucinda eyed Elton over Megan's head, stroking the baby's wispy, black hair. "Don't you dare go home to that tyrant," she said. "I can tell you're thinking about it."

It was an argument they'd been having since the telephone message from Randall, Elton's brother, had been slipped under their door. "Come home," it said. "Pop's dying." Elton had wanted to call the States immediately, but the huge time change confused him. He understood that it was a different day back home, but couldn't remember if it was yesterday or tomorrow. The East Coast was thirteen hours behind China, the operator explained when he gave in and asked for help; he scribbled on the bed-side notepad, trying to visualize the distance from Rugglesville, Virginia to their stuffy room in the White Swan Hotel overlooking the Pearl River in Guangzhou, China. Not a different day, after all: it was night where he was, so it must be the same day at home, just a lot earlier. Finally, something made sense.

"He's my father, Lu," Elton said.

"And she's our daughter."

"Not everyone agrees with that, I guess." Elton turned to stare out the window at flashing neon.

Lucinda blew her nose, setting the baby off again. "You say that like it's my fault."

They'd done everything by the book, starting more than a year ago, almost two, Elton figured, from that day they first met with the social worker. They'd had check-ups and a home study; they'd copied tax returns and paid the fees, a lot of money for a mechanic and an elementary school teacher. They'd shipped the bundle of papers to China, like so many box tops they were sending off for a prize. Then—after the prickly wait that reminded Elton of boyhood days when it seemed Christmas, and the promised sled or bike or .22, would never come—the letter arrived from the agency, with a snapshot of the baby clipped to the corner. That momentous day was followed by passports and visas—neither Elton nor Lucinda had been out of the country before, except for Elton's Gulf War stint—credit card-maxing plane tickets, gathering hand-me-down sleepers and toys, and, eventually, the flight half-way around the world. Now, after they'd leaped so many hurdles and traveled so far, it had come down to this: one piece of paper that should have been signed by the mayor in Megan's home village was missing, or mistranslated, or misdated. Elton was no longer sure exactly what had derailed them, only that they were sitting in a tiny hotel room the week before Christmas, in a country that didn't even know what the holiday was about, the whole damn process was jammed like a gummy transmission, Lucinda and Megan were wailing, and Elton had to bite his tongue.

"I didn't say it was your fault, honey."

"You didn't have to. I know you, Elton Hoffman."

"It's nobody's fault. Lawrence will fix it."

Lawrence was the adoption agency's local facilitator, and his real name was Zhengxuan, unpronounceable for Elton, who was grateful when the young man had volunteered an easy alternative. The Chinese had handed Megan over gladly; it was a paperwork-hound in the U.S. consulate who caught the fatal defect. "No problem, Mr. Elton," Lawrence had said, his ever-present smile beaming as he explained what had happened. They'd find the paper, Lawrence promised. Elton and Lucinda had heard horror stories of adoptions thwarted by missing punctuation, and here they were lacking an entire document. Elton saw the specter of an empty-handed homecoming.

Elton and Lucinda had rushed into marriage. Just back in town after college in Blacksburg, she was teaching second-graders, had student loans to pay, and hoped Fisher's Garage could make her decade-old Jetta last awhile longer. He was still living with his folks, learning his trade at Fisher's, drifting toward enlistment. She was exotic and educated; he was rugged and funny. They eloped during her Christmas break, and just a few weeks later he was off to Parris Island. Ever since, their married life had been one disappointment after another: Elton sick and out of work when he came back from the Gulf; Lucinda battling his parents, who still hadn't warmed to her, suspicious of her dark complexion and absent father; and, of course, the struggle to make a family. "It's now or never," Lucinda had said more than once. And Elton went along, even though he wasn't sure he was ready. Doctors. Pricey treatments. They'd managed to conceive twice, and both times, a few weeks in, he came home from the garage to find Lucinda curled on the bed, weeping into a pillow.

Elton's parents were against adoption from the beginning. Elton and Lucinda had moved in with them the first time Elton was laid off, giving up their rented trailer, and stayed on the farm to build a nest egg, which seemed to make the old folks think they had a say in everything—what time Elton and Lucinda came home from Rocky's Tavern, the length of Lucinda's skirts, which Church they attended, even the brand of Elton's smokes. Elton's father thought of adoption as bringing a stranger into the house, and strangers meant trouble. "Who can say what blood is in a baby's veins?" he'd asked, speaking to Elton but looking at Lucinda. Elton's mother, meticulously dusting her collection of bird figurines, had nodded, as she always did to her husband's pronouncements, and said, "You can never be too careful."

Their opposition stiffened when Elton told them he and Lucinda were adopting from China. Martin Hoffman had fought in the Korean War, had taken shrapnel in his hip when Chinese troops attacked at Chosin Reservoir, and everything Chinese galled him— from the labels in half his work shirts to the plates on the dinner table. And now there'd be one under his roof? Elton's father spluttered whenever the subject came up, and burrowed into his TV chair. His mother wrung her hands at the sink and gazed out the window.

Part of Elton had felt the same way. He didn't dare breathe a word of it to Lucinda, but it was only human, wasn't it? He'd wanted his own kids, if at all; not somebody else's. He saw his high school girlfriend around town sometimes, in a minivan full of toddlers, and he wondered why he'd missed out, if he'd made a mistake. But Lucinda said even an adopted baby was a gift from God, and Elton worked at convincing himself she was right.

Now Lucinda sat next to Elton on the stiff Chinese bed, Megan's head on her shoulder, crying over for now, eyes closed. Elton took Megan's tiny hand in his.

"I know you think you have to go," Lucinda whispered, "but you don't. There's nothing you can do for him. Your mom's there. He's got doctors."

"That's not the point."

"What *is* the point?"

Elton wished his parents could have come along, could have been there when he walked into that hotel lobby in Nanning, bleary from travel and anticipation, and saw the trio of white-coated women, one holding a sleeping infant on her lap. Surely that would have changed their minds. Elton and Lucinda had dropped their luggage and stepped forward, and the women in white rose together with grace that struck Elton as angelic. Lucinda's tears had begun the minute she saw those women, but Elton's held off until Megan was in his arms.

Her name wasn't technically Megan, of course. Not yet. They'd put that on all the forms, Megan Byrd Hoffman, Byrd after Lucinda's mother's family, but just between themselves they still called her Ling-Ling, the name penciled on the back of that first snapshot. After they arrived in China they found out it meant "double zero" if said the wrong sing-song way, "clever and nimble" if done right. How was he supposed to know which was which? "It makes her sound like some panda in the zoo," Lucinda had said. Still, when they lay on the bed that first night together, the baby between them while they tickled her and cooed and tried to make her smile, it was "Ling-Ling," they whispered.

The canned Christmas carols seemed louder now and Megan's eyes fluttered open.

"Don't let him do this to us," Lucinda said.

"It's not like he had a heart attack on purpose, for Christ's sake."

Lucinda glared.

They'd been packed, luggage piled in the front hall, one suitcase with baby clothes and diapers and stuffed animals and formula, and they paced the dining room waiting for Elton's brother. Randall had promised to drive them over the mountain to Charlottesville, where they'd catch the shuttle to Washington and then on to

Chicago, Hong Kong, Nanning. He was late, which made them worry he'd fallen off the wagon one more time, and Elton asked his father to take them, a long haul for a man who, just shy of seventy, rarely drove at all anymore. But if they missed the Hong Kong flight, the best they could do was catch the same flight the next day, and that was no sure thing so close to the holidays. What choice did they have? Elton's mother shook her head and disappeared into the kitchen.

Despite being against the whole enterprise, the old man had pulled on his field coat, stretched to lace up his boots, and that's when the pain started, shooting down his arm, he said, although Elton saw it in his twisted face. Randall finally showed up, wobbly, about the same time as the ambulance, so Elton drove his brother and their mother to the hospital, keeping pace with that ambulance, and no benefit of sirens and flashing lights. The flight missed, Lucinda stewed at home.

In the emergency room, Elton's father seemed fine—more tired than sick. "Take me home," he'd grumped, as soon as the flurry of tests had ended. They weren't letting him loose that easily, though, and Elton's mother stayed behind while Elton and Randall headed back. Elton seethed at the wheel, worried about Lucinda and their plane tickets and the baby, but Randall wouldn't stop talking. He rambled on about how God was watching over Pop and it just wasn't his time, how the old man looked good, considering, and didn't Elton want to put off his foolish baby-buying trip until Pop was up and about?

"Brother, you'd better shut up," Elton said.

"And you, *Brother*, had better get your head on straight. You're killing him."

Lucinda was on the porch when they got to the house, smoking, which she hadn't done in three years despite Elton's refusal to quit. She stubbed out her cigarette in the ashtray cupped in her hand. Elton and Randall climbed out of the Jeep, and Elton thought his brother might get right back in and drive off when he saw Lucinda's scowl. Elton almost felt sorry for him.

"What in God's name got into you?" Lucinda shouted, even before they reached the steps.

"Just a little Christmas party," Randall said. "Ho Ho Ho."

"We've been planning this for months. You know how important it is. Wreck your own life if you want, drink yourself to death, I don't give a damn. But leave my family out of it!" She wasn't wrong, and Elton let her blow.

The hotel room smelled sour and stale; the ceiling light flickered; Elton's head ached. Lucinda paced with Megan in her arms, both quiet for the time being, but Elton saw how red and puffy his wife's eyes were. Finally, he figured out how to use his credit card to call, and dialed the numbers. He listened to the ringing on the other end.

"No answer," he said.

"Your mother's probably at the hospital," Lucinda said. Megan's head was poised on Lucinda's shoulder, eyes shut, mouth open in a perfect little o.

He dialed again, Randall's number this time, and waited. His brother's voice was hoarse, words slurred.

"Jesus, Randall, drink your breakfast?"

"Screw you."

"How's Pop?"

"Had a big one this time. Not doing good."

"What's that mean?"

"You shouldn't have left."

Lucinda was right about his father being a tyrant, Elton had to admit, at least when it came to her. He'd sit in his TV chair and shout, "Girl, get me some tea," or "Do something about them filthy windows." She took it and boiled and let Elton know when they were alone that it wasn't right, that he should stand up for her. Both Elton and Randall had it tough as kids, too; the old man worked them hard on the farm, wasn't afraid to use the strap when he didn't like something they did or said. Randall would have been better off if he'd left home, joined the service like Elton, instead of staying under their father's thumb. It hadn't been all bad, though, not all the time. Lucinda just didn't see the whole picture. The old man was good to their mother, raised his voice to her now and then but never his hand. When Elton and Randall were boys he made sure they had what they needed, made sure Christmas was all they hoped for. He taught them how to hunt and fish, drilled them in the simple virtues: honesty and hard work. Elton had always thought his father would live forever, a down-home Methuselah.

Elton needed to get home.

Damn it, though, they couldn't leave, not until Megan was officially theirs, not until all the t's were crossed, and that meant waiting for Lawrence to get that missing paper and hoping the consulate would reschedule them sometime soon, take pity on them, if the bureaucrats even knew such a concept.

"Honey," he said, choosing his words carefully, "I need to go back." He stared at the phone, at the swan etched into the notepad, thought of his mother's collection of lifeless birds, and couldn't look at Lucinda. It wouldn't be easy by herself, but she was smart and strong; she could deal with the consulate. He didn't care if the old man was a tyrant. His father needed him.

"Elton." His name, spoken once, sharply, to drill through whatever interference was going on in his head. "It's not an option. We need you here."

"What if I don't get to say goodbye? What if he—"

"This is the future, Elton." She held out the baby to him, and Megan settled snugly into his arms.

Elton couldn't sleep. A vision of his father, frightened and pale, attached to tubes and wires, wouldn't leave him. He slipped out of bed. In the green glow of streetlights he packed a suitcase. Megan stirred in her crib and he went to her, stroked her feathery hair with his finger. He lifted her up and cradled her. "Ling-Ling," he whispered. In her sleep she sucked; her breath was light and even.

In the morning, while Lucinda showered, Elton unpacked. After breakfast, even without all the paperwork in hand, they completed as many of the final steps as they could. At a clinic near the consulate, an efficient Chinese doctor examined Megan, poked and prodded and took chest x-rays, and pronounced her healthy. Elton studied the document she gave them, covered in official, bright-red chops, like Christmas bows, and wondered again how anyone could make out what the words meant. They strolled along the street facing the White Swan, explored the tourist shops decked out in plastic pine trees and garlands, bought souvenirs for his family: a postcard for Randall with his name in Chinese characters, something to amuse the regulars at Rocky's Tavern; a gold-plated monkey for his father; a porcelain swan from the hotel gift shop for his mother.

Lawrence phoned. The official who needed to sign the missing document was himself missing, perhaps at a Communist Party meeting, no one was sure where, maybe Beijing. Another day lost and Elton lay awake that night, too, revisited by his father. He thought of repacking, heading to the airport right then to find whatever flight he could, knowing that his father expected it of him, but he heard the baby's soft breathing and knew he couldn't go.

The following day, Lawrence called again. The Mayor had returned, the paper had been signed and the official chops affixed. It would arrive in Guangzhou on Saturday, maybe Sunday. Lawrence would reschedule the interview with the consulate for Monday. No problem. Tuesday, at the latest. Then they'd be free to head home, two days before Christmas. Christmas Eve-eve, Elton's mother called it, and remembering that made him smile.

"It's all set," Elton told Lucinda. "No more surprises. You can handle it."

Lucinda cradled Megan in her arms and glared at Elton. "If you leave now, there's nothing to handle. This is all a huge mistake."

"Baby, you're not being fair. You're asking me to choose between him and you."

She kissed Megan's forehead. "Not just me."

Elton called the airline to change their flight. There were no seats, not even in business class, which, despite the crazy expense, Elton thought to check. He recalled the wider seats upfront on the way over. "Nothing in first class, either," said the ticket agent, although that impossibility hadn't occurred to him.

"We have to get home," Elton said meekly, feeling his last chance slip away.

"There's nothing. Unless you try standby."

There was no answer at home, even though it was the middle of the night in Virginia. He imagined his mother sitting in a stiff chair in his father's hospital room, one dim lamp glowing over the romance novel she was reading, or maybe it was the Bible, while his father slept. Maybe she'd strung Christmas lights on the bed, a wreath on the window. He called Randall, who should have been home asleep at that hour. No answer. Elton left a message, the flight they hoped to be on, arrival time. "Meet us at the airport, Randall," he said to the answering machine. "Don't screw this up, Little Brother." And then, stung by the harshness of his own words, he added, "Wait till you see her."

During the rescheduled interview at the consulate, Elton held Megan. Lucinda's hands were folded in her lap, but she fidgeted— first with Megan's pacifier, then, when the baby needed it, with the clasp on her purse. Mr. Jamison, the consular officer, a stout, balding man with a bushy moustache, opened the file folder and scrutinized each document, ran his finger down the middle and stopped at signatures, nodded, and moved on. He made a stack next to the folder and straightened the corners each time he added a finished page. He reached the end of the folder and shook his head.

Lucinda reached for Elton's hand.

Jamison turned the stack over, shuffled through the documents again. "Here it is," he said. He looked up at them and nodded. "Usually that one's at the end." He rearranged the papers, and closed the folder.

"Everything there?" Elton asked.

"Looks like you've got yourself a daughter." Jamison grinned and Elton smiled, his whole body trembling and fluid. Lucinda brushed away tears. There was more paperwork, from the consulate's side this time, and Jamison explained each of the new documents, papers they would need to leave China and pass through Hong

Kong and enter the U.S., papers they would need when applying for the baby's citizenship once they got home.

Jamison stood. Elton and Lucinda stood. Megan squirmed. They all shook hands and Jamison pulled a candy cane out of a basket on his desk and presented it to Elton. "I guess she's too young for this, but . . . Merry Christmas."

II.

From the Chinese airline captain at the Guangzhou airport who comforted squealing Megan while Lucinda dug in her purse for the passports and tickets ("May I?" he asked with outstretched arms, and then sang softly to the baby in Chinese), to the silver-haired Oklahoma gentleman at the Hong Kong check-in counter who gave up his seats on the Chicago flight while his plump wife fussed over the baby, and Craig, the flight attendant who, somewhere over the Pacific, mercifully walked the aisles of the 747 with Megan while Elton and Lucinda ate and rested, the trip home passed in a blur of miracles. Elton closed his eyes and allowed himself to imagine Megan basking in his father's welcoming embrace, his mother's blissful glow.

As they approached Chicago, the pilot announced that during the night a blizzard had dumped a foot of snow on the city, but the sun was shining now and O'Hare's runways had been cleared. More good fortune, and Elton was grateful. When the flight for Washington took off, only a few minutes late, they had a glorious view of the Loop skyscrapers and the radiant city, still and white, the dark lake stretching endlessly north and east. The flight attendants wore Santa hats and led the passengers in singing carols.

They landed at Dulles under dense, numbing skies, the passage into the terminal frigid and reeking of jet exhaust. Their next connection, the shuttle to Charlottesville, was scheduled to leave from the narrow mid-field building, filled with college kids on their way home for the holidays and one boisterous group with tattered lift-tickets dangling from ski-jackets. When Elton found the gate and checked in, the agent cast a wary eye to the dim window.

"There's snow down there. Snow's everywhere now, except here. Only a matter of time."

The loudspeaker announced flight delays and cancellations. One of the skiers pounded his fist on the check-in counter and shouted at the agent. Lucinda, eyes half-closed, entertained Megan with a plush rabbit. Elton crossed his arms and paced, head buzzing and gut aching from the long flight. He discovered a smokers' lounge but stayed only a few minutes. He found a phone, left another message for Randall, resumed pacing.

"Ladies and Gentlemen," the agent's voice squawked through the public address system, "if we don't board this flight right this minute, you're not going anywhere."

The eighteen-seat prop-jet filled and, with the barest of pre-flight ritual, climbed into the air, not much more than crop-duster high. Lucinda hugged Megan to her chest. Elton watched frozen brown furrows give way to rolling horse country, and then the ground turned white and so did the swirling sky. He could see nothing, and over the whining engines he could hear nothing. Then the short flight was over, they were headed down, shaking and fish-tailing. He reached across the narrow aisle to grip Lucinda's hand.

When they stepped onto the icy tarmac, the wintry blast overwhelmed Elton's nylon jacket and Lucinda's denim vest, all they'd packed for the pleasant nights of subtropical Southern China. At least Megan looked snug in her snow-white parka.

There was no sign of Randall, not that Elton was surprised. He hunted for a phone, wondering if cabs were running in that weather, if one would take them over the mountain to Rugglesville, and how much that would cost. Elton stepped outside and a wet gust nearly slapped him back. Snow had piled on parked cars, tires and windshields buried. He saw one car skid into a stop sign. Another inched away from the airport on a snow-hidden road.

"Not much moving out there," he said when he was back inside. They'd come so far to be with his father, and now it looked as if they couldn't make it the last few miles. Elton could barely look at Lucinda. If only she had let him leave. "One day makes a difference."

"You're blaming me for the snowstorm?"

"Jesus. I didn't say that."

The airport's single conveyer lurched, and luggage streamed by; Elton jumped to grab theirs. Each time he added a bag to their collection he looked at the door, thinking he'd have Randall in his sights, that soon they'd be on their way to the hospital. Finally they had all the suitcases, but no Randall.

"He's not coming," Lucinda said. She didn't sound angry or disappointed, just tired. "Let's find a motel."

"No, damn it." His voice was too loud. He heard the anger in it, knew that people were watching. He took a breath. "You don't . . . you can't understand. I have to get there."

Lucinda had been raised by her mother and grandparents after her father—an itinerant who had stopped in town just long enough—disappeared, before there was a wedding, before she was born. In college, with what little her mother had told her, she'd made an attempt to find him, poring over phone books in the library and following the slimmest of leads, but came up empty. She had confided in Elton, when he proposed, that she hoped his father might fill the void. That just made the old man's hostility all the more hurtful.

"I mean," Elton said, "we can't stop now."

He faced the cold again. Storm-blurred headlights approached, tires creaked on fresh snow, and a Jeep slowed to a stop. Randall's Jeep. Randall jumped out, and slid toward Elton.

"You had to come home during the storm of the century," he said, grinning.

"Brother, I'm glad to see you," Elton said, arms around Randall, sniffing for beer. Elton stepped back, peered into Randall's clear eyes, hugged him again.

He pulled his brother inside the terminal. Randall brushed the snow from his hair and leaned to kiss the baby, but Lucinda backed away; he chuckled and shook his head. Elton put suitcases in his hands and the two of them loaded the Jeep, settling the diaper bag, with the carefully wrapped swan and the monkey for his father, next to Lucinda in the back seat. Elton headed Randall off when he went for the driver's side. He was pleased that Randall was in a sober phase—he wondered, briefly, what the cause of the transformation might be—and grateful for one more favor on this long road home, but now he needed to be in control. He took the keys.

"How's Pop?" Elton asked.

"We'd best head to the hospital directly."

"Elton," said Lucinda. His name, sharply, one time.

He looked at Lucinda and the baby, then at Randall. "Can we swing home first?"

"Honest, I don't think so," Randall said.

Elton wanted to shout at Lucinda that he should have come home sooner, that she shouldn't have stopped him, that they were too late now and it was her fault, maybe adoption wasn't such a good idea after all, the old man was his father for Christ's sake and why did she have to come between them all the time? But Randall was there watching him. And the baby was asleep. And it was still snowing. And Elton was so tired. He gripped the steering wheel, hard, so that the bones of his hands hurt—a trick his father had taught him—and he felt his anger cool.

He looked at Lucinda in the rearview mirror. "We're going to the hospital."

Heading away from the airport, even the Jeep struggled on the long, slick grades, and they passed more than one stranded vehicle: a Town Car spinning its wheels, drifting backwards; a Toyota in a ditch, its swerving tracks already covered by new snow; a Pontiac stopped dead in the middle of the road, abandoned. Things were better on the interstate, as the highway crews had managed to clear one lane each way, but Elton knew at some point they'd pass those crews and run into a mess on the mountain. Snow was still falling, and he could barely see out the window.

It was slow going. Lucinda's eyes pleaded with him in the mirror. As a kid he'd seen that dark pool in his mother's eyes whenever the sky turned black with clouds, or the wind roared through the treetops. He knew Lucinda feared for them all, even for his idiot brother Randall, who for once had not disappointed them, but mostly she feared for the baby. And he knew she wanted to get home and rock Megan by the fire, and sing to her, and show her the tree, and teach her about Christmas and being part of a family.

They passed the road crews. Elton felt the Jeep drift sideways, aware that nothing he did affected where they went. Then the front tires caught a dry patch and the Jeep went into a spin, and at least that was something Elton could handle. He gripped the wheel, turned into the spin and they moved forward again.

The wipers brushed snow across the windshield, leaving icy trails. Elton concentrated on the dark road and the snow in the headlights, but saw his father. There was still hope, wasn't there? Wouldn't his father hang on, knowing Elton was on the way? Wouldn't his mother tell him to wait?

When Elton was seven, Randall had scarlet fever. Elton was forbidden to enter his brother's room, the room they shared, and for weeks slept on the couch; his father rarely came inside the house at all, preferring the barn or the fields. But Elton watched his mother care for Randall, toting water pails into the room to bathe him, staying for hours to read to him, leaving with bedding and clothes to be disinfected. When the contagion had passed and Randall's fever had broken, Elton's father presented her with a whittled mallard, the first in her collection.

An eighteen-wheeler roared past, causing Elton to steer right, out of the packed snow. When he did that, he couldn't change course again, couldn't turn back into the road, couldn't do anything, and they slid off the highway. He heard a swallowed gasp from Lucinda, curses from Randall as he banged his head on the window. They twirled around and then to the side and Elton threw his arm behind him thinking he could keep Lucinda and the baby from flying forward if they hit something or rolled, and finally the Jeep thudded to a stop in the ditch, tilting right, like a wind-beaten sapling.

Elton heard the deep-woods stillness, and for a moment they just sat there. He thought of his father in the silent hospital room, and his mother at bedside. When Elton had come back from the Gulf, with the headaches and tiredness, dizzy spells and shortness of breath, the disease the VA hospital denied existed and wouldn't treat, it was his mother who nursed him while Lucinda worked, his father who urged him onto his feet.

Randall moaned and held his hands to his head.

"Shit." Elton pounded the steering wheel.

"This baby needs to get home," Lucinda said.

"We'll get you home." Elton saw the trickle of blood on his brother's forehead.

"You need to get to the hospital to see Pop," Randall said.

"I know I do." Elton looked at Lucinda.

"Take us home."

Lucinda stayed in the Jeep with the baby while Elton surveyed their predicament with Randall. The wind bit into Elton's back, and snow pricked his ears. He jammed his hands in his pockets and knelt by the buried rear wheel. Randall pointed at the deep rut and shook his head.

"Let's try," Elton said.

Randall shook his head again. "Not without a tow."

"You want us to sit here and freeze to death?"

They climbed back into the Jeep and ran the heater. Elton kept his eyes on the road, his head numb with fatigue.

Headlights approached, coming up the slope, appearing to blink in the waves of blowing snow. Elton jumped out and ran onto the highway, waving his arms over his head.

The car, a black Explorer, didn't slow, but the passenger's side window came down.

"Stop up there," Elton yelled, pointing to the hill's crest, and the passenger responded with thumbs up.

Elton and Randall herded Lucinda and the baby out of the car, snow feathering all their heads, and began the slog up the hill in the Explorer's tracks. Lucinda made Elton run back to the Jeep for the bag with the diapers and formula.

The Explorer waited at the top of the grade, steam puffing out the rear, taillights glowing softly through the snow like Christmas ornaments. They cleared space in the back seat and set off. Although the Explorer had reached the top of that particular hill, there was a descent to come and yet another climb before they were across the mountain. Jud, the driver, clenched the wheel and concentrated on the road. Lucinda leaned into Elton and held his arm.

"It's all about momentum," Jud said as they topped the ridge and started down the western slope. "Can't get anywhere without momentum."

"Elton," Lucinda said.

Elton cradled Megan and whispered to her, "We're going to see your Grandpa, Ling-Ling, Grandma and Grandpa are going to love our little Ling-Ling."

Randall led the way to Intensive Care, nearly at a jog, pulling Elton with him. When they came to their father's room, Randall stood aside and let Elton pass. Their mother sat at the bedside, bathed in gray light. Snow pelted the window. Her hand clutched the old man's hand.

"Mom," Elton said. "We're here." His head pounded, his tongue felt rough, and he could smell his own stink. "We made it."

His mother turned, just enough to acknowledge their presence without losing sight of Elton's father. She lifted his hand and touched it to her lips, then settled it back on the sheet. Elton could see she was taking deep breaths. She stood, and let Elton embrace her.

"He asked for you." Her voice was hoarse, but even, her eyes dry.

Elton looked to the hulking monitors above his father's bed, silent, off. The room seemed to spin. God damn it, he'd wanted to come home. Lucinda should have let him, she could have handled it, could have traveled on her own with the baby, he should have been there for his father, who had been there for him when it mattered, he should have fixed what was broken between them, he should have made his father accept Lucinda and the baby. It was Lucinda's fault. He'd tried to do the right thing. He'd tried to do what everyone else wanted.

"You weren't here." His mother turned back to the bed.

He didn't know if she'd even seen Megan. It wasn't as if he hadn't tried. It wasn't his fault. But there was the baby to think about. They'd brought her the baby and the damn white swan for her collection. He'd tried. The baby was right there and she didn't even look.

"You weren't here," Randall said. He moved to the bed, stroked their father's arm. Tears streamed down his cheeks and he brushed them away with the back of his hand. Elton moved behind Randall and put his hands on his brother's shoulders. Randall twisted free.

Elton looked to Lucinda, who stood in the harsh light from the hall with Megan. He turned back and gazed at his father's face. He wanted to watch the old man's eyes open and see Megan's smile. He wanted to put the baby in his arms. He wanted the old man to open his heart to her, to Lucinda and the baby both, to make up for everything. He was sorry he was late. He was tired and dizzy and sorry.

"It's Elton, Pop," he said. "We're back."

He wanted to tell his father about holding Megan in his arms for the first time and understanding what it meant to be a father, to start a family, about the Christmas carols in China and what a surprise it was, about the White Swan hotel.

"I tried to get here sooner."

He wanted his mother to take the baby from Lucinda and sing to her and rock her and look into her eyes. He wanted to give her the porcelain swan and have her love it and praise it. He wanted Lucinda to forgive him and to understand and to tell him it didn't matter and that everything was okay. He wanted Randall to stay sober and turn the corner and lead his own life. He wanted Megan to be safe and happy. And he wanted to sleep. He wanted desperately to sleep.

SAVAGE SOURCE

We live in an old chaos of the sun . . .
—from Sunday Morning by Wallace Stevens

Peeking between the sheet halves that covered her bedroom window, Tina waited for Ben. She ached to be with him, to touch him.

But wasn't it all the rushing that had ruined things the first time? Hadn't her mother always said—as if it were practically a Commandment—that a girl should hold something back? She'd been too eager before, too desperate. She was to blame for everything.

So now, when he pulled up in front of her place just after eleven and parked his grumbling pickup in the halo of a streetlamp, she made herself slow down. She took a deep breath, watched him climb out of the truck and cross the street, listened for his footsteps on the walk and then the porch steps, and only then did she allow herself to move. She dawdled on the stairs, took them one at a time, held firmly to the banister, checked her hair in the hall mirror, and straightened her tank top before dragging open the heavy, oak door.

But then there he was, grinning and panting on the wide stoop, smelling dark and subterranean, like the coffee house where he worked. She threw her arms around his neck and smashed her mouth on his before he'd even had a chance to say, "Hi."

"Hi," he said when she finally let him breathe.

In the truck, Ben was quiet as he drove and didn't say where they were going even when she asked. He just looked over at her once in a while as if to make sure she was still there. Wood smoke drifted through the open windows. The night sky was dense.

They'd met only the week before. Tina had been in line behind Pam at Java Mountain, the single decent coffee place in shriveled-up Rugglesville. She'd noticed how her friend's jeans slid down her narrow hips, and how the new tattoo just above her butt crack looked like a fistful of knives. Tina's father and stepmother would kill her if she did anything like that, even though Tina'd been on her own for months, since the day she turned 18, announced that she would no longer answer to the name Melissa, and moved into the dilapidated Victorian with Pam. It was going to be bad enough when her over-protective father got a load of the new hair color, a neon pink that even Tina had doubts about. It wasn't as if she'd joined a cult or anything, not like that Shifflet girl who'd married a stranger alongside a thousand other couples in a football stadium. Still, Tina's dad would freak.

Java Mountain's artwork had changed since her last visit. There'd been black and white photographs before, austere portraits and sleepy street scenes; now, sprawling canvases covered the walls, mesmerizing abstracts that made no sense. Tina liked their gutsy yellows and oranges, though, until she noticed, concealed in the chaos of each one, a shadowy, blood-red cross. That reminded her too much of her mother—her certifiably nuts, lies-through-her-teeth, claims-to-have-found-Jesus mother.

Country music twanged above the hum of the coffee grinder. The line moved. A woman at the front who was a dead-ringer for Tina's stepmother—flowered dress, crucifix broach, stiff, swirled hair that looked like cotton candy and smelled like bug spray—was saying to the young guy behind the counter, you're Ben Craig . . . John Craig's boy. Tina watched him work the milk steamer: long skinny arms, like Q-tips, snake tattoo above his wrist, a pimple glowing through black chin stubble, silver ring in his eyebrow. Doing fine, Ma'am, he was saying, been gone, but now I'm back. His shoulder blades heaved under his white t-shirt when he twisted the espresso filter into place.

Pam ordered the fancy stuff, with caramel and whipped cream. She earned big tips at the nail salon and, on top of that, scored an allowance from her dad—a long-haul trucker who felt guilty for running off with a girl barely a year older than Pam—so she could afford it. With what Mrs. Stuckey paid her at the gift shop, even boring regular coffee was a stretch for Tina.

She took Pam's place at the counter, and there was that Ben or whatever, looking right at her with his searing, bloodshot eyes.

"What can I get you?" His voice was raspy and thin. He wore holey jeans, and his black hair was buzzed short. Tina wanted to rub it, to see if it was feathery like her baby cousin's, or scratchy, the way she remembered her dad's face when she was little, before her mom grabbed her off the porch one day and kept her running for years, lying to her about her father, lying about everything. Not that she blamed her mother for bolting out of Rugglesville, not when bolting was all Tina could think about.

"Miss?"

She ordered. He pumped her coffee and stood patiently, not drumming his fingers or anything, while Tina counted out the nickels and dimes. She wanted to make a joke about the coins, how she'd been digging under sofa cushions all week, but she felt him watching and couldn't think.

"I like your hair," Ben said.

Tina came back to Java Mountain on her lunch break. She peered in the window and saw Ben behind the counter, but didn't go inside. What would she say? She had no more change. She sat on the curb and lit a cigarette. She fluffed her pink hair. She pulled a thread from the fresh rip in her jeans.

And then there he was, crouched next to her.

"I saw you look in," he said.

"Me?" she asked, aiming for aloof, afraid she'd missed. She puffed on the cigarette and stared up at the clouds, into the street, anywhere but at him. Half a Styrofoam cup tumbled by.

When she got home, Pam was in the kitchen, reading the

directions on a box of macaroni and cheese. Blue flames licked the pan of water.

"I think he's the one," said Tina. "Just like my mom predicted. It's spooky." Tina's mother worked the checkout at Wal-Mart but told fortunes on the side, a talent she'd picked up on the run, in Iowa or Arizona, and hadn't abandoned even for Jesus.

"Whacked, more like," Pam said. She stirred the pot. "You believe that hooey?"

"Mom says it's destiny." Not that Tina ever listened to her mother, or even saw her much. Her father didn't approve and kept a close watch, which is why she'd had to get out of his house. "She said she could see it in my palm, a marked man in my future. And sure enough he's got this sweet snake tattoo on his arm."

"It's just a tattoo, girl. It doesn't mean he's your savior."

"But he could be, right?" Tina gulped the wine in Pam's glass, then unscrewed the cap and filled a coffee mug for herself. A drop trickled down the bottle and bled onto the counter. "What if he's the one?"

The truck careened along a winding road.

"My place—my dad's place—is up ahead," Ben said.

Tina imagined them doing it in Ben's narrow bed, shelves of his boyhood trophies and rock-star posters as witness. They came upon the house, a brick ranch, its windows dark, and sped past. She moved closer to him, put her hand on his thigh, and pictured new possibilities—a motel, a deserted park, a cozy tent in the woods.

For their first date, Tina and Ben had arranged to meet at the Ice Dream after she got off work at the Bazaar. They sat in a booth by the window, with a view of Main Street, on sticky vinyl benches. She noticed that people stared at them, as if they were both naked, or wore tall white turbans, but figured, most likely, it was because of her pink hair. She'd decided she liked it after all. It showed she couldn't care less what those small-town Jesus freaks thought. You acted a little different, you tried to think for yourself for once in your life, and they looked at you like you shot the Pope.

"My gig at the gift shop is temporary," she said. "I'm sure as hell not going to spend the rest of my life selling ceramic doodads to porky tourists."

Ben reached across the table and wiped a smear of chocolate from her cheek. His soft touch surprised her, not because he hadn't seemed gentle in the short time they'd known each other, but because no boy had ever touched her like that.

"It's just until I can save enough for cosmetology school," she went on, her gaze fixed on Ben's dark eyes. "I'll probably go down to Roanoke. I bet I could have my own salon there in, like, five years. I'd do anything to get out of this hole."

Ben nodded. "It's like they're watching every second. Won't let you move."

Tina wasn't sure—was he talking about the losers in the ice cream place?—but she nodded back.

"I'm sick of everyone telling me what to think," he said. "My dad, his church. It's too much. And if you don't swallow it, if they hear this much hesitation in your voice,"—he held his thumb and forefinger up for her to see, with just a sliver of light between them—"they treat you like you're the one they'll blame for the next flood."

"Exactly," Tina said, leaning across the table. He was so perfect, saying exactly what she'd been thinking, that she couldn't breathe. "What does it matter what happened thousands of years ago? It's like somebody made it all up to control us. So we'd, like, owe them."

"I really do owe them," he said, lowering his eyes. "Money."

"That's not quite what I—"

"There was this jackass from New Jersey? On shore leave? In this bar down in Norfolk? Ragging me about some southern redneck shit and pitched a cue ball through the window like he thought he was Roger Clemens. Man, there was glass all over, broken sticks. Beat the crap out of that asshole, so they tagged me for everything. It's never the guy who starts it who gets blamed, you know? Even booted me out of the Navy. Like I give a shit."

Ben told her how his dad had borrowed from his church to

cover the damage, made a big deal about being disappointed in Ben. How he'd let everyone down. The congregation. God. Now every little screw-up—two DUIs in one month, bounced out of the Y after a brawl on the basketball court—pulled the ropes tighter.

"Soon as it's paid off I'm out of there. It'll be, 'Adios, Dad.' I'll make my own way."

Tina waited for him to go on, but Ben lit a cigarette and just gazed at her. He rubbed his silver eyebrow ring, as if making a wish.

"I know all about lousy dads," she said, thinking his didn't sound so awful. She wondered if hers would have bailed her out like that. More likely, he'd lock her in a closet. "What about your mom?"

"Not a true believer, apparently." He snorted, and smoke rolled across the table.

Gone? Dead? What? Tina put her hand on his, expecting more, but he pulled away. She scraped the last of the chocolate sauce out of the pink plastic sundae dish between them.

"You want to hang at Rocky's, shoot some pool? A guy I know tends bar weekends. We could maybe score some drinks."

"Let's not," Tina said, pleased with the disappointment she saw in his eyes. "I mean, I can't. They card, right?" Tina's excellent fake driver's license practically throbbed in her wallet, just behind the real one. But she was a little too well known at Rocky's, which Ben didn't need to learn just yet. "Why don't you get us a six-pack, and we'll head back to my place?"

Ben was digging in his jeans pocket for the truck keys before she'd finished the invitation. Tina leaned against him as they hurried through the Ice Dream's parking lot. Ben looped his arm around her shoulder. Her arm circled his hips.

When they got to her house, she flew through the foyer, tugging Ben with her. They ran up the steps to her bedroom. Nothing was going to stop her. This was her destiny. Her mother had said the marked man would take her away, and Tina couldn't wait for the prophecy to come true. If Ben was her ticket out, then she was ready to board the train.

She closed her bed-sheet curtain—not for privacy but to hide the pink panties she'd hung in the window to dry. She pulled her stuffed Pooh from the pillow and clutched him in her lap, her mind racing ahead, already giving herself to Ben, packing a suitcase, moving on with him to their future. Ben popped open two cans and they sat on the edge of the sagging twin bed. She sipped hers, gazing at him over the lip of the can; he gulped his. Their knees collided, and she moved her leg so they touched the length of their thighs, fitting together perfectly, like two pieces of a human puzzle. The thought made her giggle, and, when she turned away to hide it, Ben planted his mouth on her neck, dropped his empty beer can on the shag, and clamped his hand on her breast.

Tina flung Pooh in the direction of the closet. Ben slipped his hand beneath her t-shirt. She moaned, more out of encouragement than ecstasy, turned her head toward him with lips apart, and leaned back on her elbows. He pushed his face into hers; their tongues dueled. His hand crawled higher under her shirt, and he lay on top of her, squirming and kissing. Then her t-shirt flew off, and they struggled together to unhook her bra. He cupped her breasts in his hands; she lifted his t-shirt, made him raise his arms so she could peel it away; she dug her nails into his chest, pushed him back and followed through to land on top. She leaned to kiss him. He tasted of cigarettes and beer and chocolate. She didn't stop him when he curled a finger in the waist of her jeans, unbuckled the belt, undid the snap.

Now she had a good look at him. He truly was pretty: long, fine lashes, light blue eyes like faded jeans, lips cracked and full, skin nearly as pale as her own. She pushed his hands away while she studied him, trying to learn it all before her insides blinded her. He had a beautiful hairless chest, a trail of tiny pimples down the center, a scar creeping up one side, below his sharp brown nipple. She moved her fingers to touch it but the scar was smooth, not a scar at all.

Tina swatted Ben's hands away from her zipper, grinned, and rocked on his crotch. She touched his chest as she swayed, her fingers brushing the surface at first, probing as she moved faster.

She felt Ben's whole body tense beneath her and shudder, then go slack.

Tina knew what that meant. She stopped rocking and rolled off, landing at his side. She pushed up his shoulder, drew a wide circle on his soft, decorated skin, the scar that wasn't a scar.

"What's this?" she asked.

"Just a tatt," Ben said weakly. His body was limp, and he'd curled into himself on the bed.

"I want to see," she said. "I love tattoos." It was partly to distract him—she knew not to draw attention to what had happened, a useful lesson from her mother's experience with men—but it was mostly the truth. Tattoos always revealed something; you just had to know how to read them, like her mom reading palms and cards. If she were to get one it would be a butterfly on her breast. Her dad would never know, no one would know, and it would suit Tina perfectly. She tried to twist Ben around so she could study his, but he pushed her away, so hard she nearly tumbled off the bed.

He yanked his t-shirt on, scooped up the rest of the six-pack by the plastic rings, and hurtled down the stairs.

Tina thought about going after him. She had practically thrown herself at him and would gladly have given it another try. Maybe that's what she'd done wrong. Maybe he was the kind of guy who needed to be in control, not like Dab, her last boyfriend, the dim-witted football player who'd expected her to do all the work and gave nothing back. But Ben didn't say anything! How was she supposed to know? And, anyway, if he didn't want her, that was his problem. She'd get over it. Besides, he'd only slow her down. He was stuck in this dump and she didn't want anyone holding her back. Maybe she'd get that butterfly after all. She'd find her own way out. To hell with Ben.

She'd only seen his tattoo for a minute, before he freaked. It was spectacular, like Pam's, with tongues of flame, but way bigger. It covered his whole shoulder blade, the fire licking under his arm, into the furry pit, down to the nipple, across his back to the other side. It was a roaring ball of flames so intense she'd thought it might be hot to the touch, but it was cool and smooth, like the rest of him. In the center were two bolts of lightning. It looked like that jagged Nazi symbol she remembered from some boring history class, not the crazy swastika, the other one, those paired esses. She didn't care if Ben was a Nazi, or a Jehovah's Witness, or a fucking Mormon. That stuff didn't mean anything to her. She wished he hadn't run off. She wanted to ask what the tattoo was all about, to taste it, to taste him. Shit.

Ben reached under the seat of the pickup and pulled out the remains of the six-pack they'd started on their first date. He handed Tina a warm can, held another between his knees and popped it open. He looked at her and grinned again. She wondered if he'd noticed that she'd nudged her hair color from plain-old pink to more like fuchsia.

"That purply red color—it's awesome," Ben said and drank from his can.

What else could he do besides read minds?

They sped further from town and now there were only a few farmhouses, down snaky gravel drives, soft lights glowing in upstairs windows. He drove fast, swerving into the left lane as the road bent sharply around a dense stand of pines.

"I love racing through the woods," he said. "It's like being on the ship, crashing through the ocean at night. Only good thing about the Navy. Not free, but free. Know what I mean?" He switched off the lights, and still they hurtled forward into the pitch black, on an invisible road.

She clutched the seat, braced her legs on the floor. Carefree was one thing, reckless another thing altogether. "Not really," she said.

Ben laughed yet again and went faster. He switched the lights back on.

They turned off the paved road onto a dirt track, climbing through the hills, first through a rock-studded pasture, then scrub and patchy trees, then a forest of hemlock and oak.

"Jesus, Ben. Where are you taking me?"

"A little celebration," Ben said, "with the congregation."

"I thought you hated your dad's church."

"Not my dad's. Mine. I've found what I was looking for."

He didn't seem the church type, so she knew he was joking. The Church of Good Times, maybe. The Church of Beer and Pot.

"You guys aren't into human sacrifice or anything, are you?" There was a twinkle of fear in her gut, even though the idea was ridiculous.

"Only virgins," Ben said, and turned to her with a grin.

She grinned back and loosened her grip on the seat.

The truck thudded over a rock, the seat bounced on squeaky springs, and Ben slowed. They splashed through a stream. A waterfall rumbled nearby, and the air felt cooler. Finally, the track they'd been following narrowed to a point and stopped. Ben shut off the engine and killed the lights. It was as if he'd pulled a blanket over her head.

"There's a trail," Ben said. "But it's too early. Let's sit awhile."

Tina listened to the chirr of crickets and the thumping of her own heart. An owl hooted. Her father had hooted like that when she was little, to make her laugh. It was so dark. And cold. A gust shook the trees. She wanted him to touch her. She waited. Her stomach cramped.

"About my church," Ben said. "It's not your average sort of church."

The Church of Sin. The Church of Sex.

"I know about churches," Tina said. Her knees trembled, and the shaking spread to her chest and arms. "My Grandpa was a preacher. And smoked and swore and drank. They're all hypocrites."

Although she'd been hoping for it, she flinched when he touched her neck, but then his lips brushed her cheek and the trembling stopped. She let his hands explore everywhere, guided his fingers to the clasp of her jeans, felt him probe under the elastic of her panties. And then he was gone, jumping out of the truck, leaving her breathless, mystified.

Her door opened. His hand found hers and she went with him.

She leaned back against the hood of the pickup, her toes dipping into the mud and pine needles. Ben pulled her hips forward, pressed himself to her and kissed her. The Ford's engine hissed.

"Hypocrites," Ben said, as if he'd been thinking about it while his tongue snaked inside. "That's a good word for it. My dad and everyone in his church, buried in their book. They don't see what's really important. They don't get it." He moved his hands to her breasts and kissed her again.

Tina had avoided Java Mountain after the first date disaster, but then one day Ben appeared at the Bazaar. Tina smiled when she saw him, and bounced on her toes, until she remembered she was supposed to be mad; she tried to frown. She thought he'd mention the botched sex, come up with excuses, because wasn't that what men did? Instead, he launched in another direction: home-schooled, they tried to make me think like them, Mom fed-up with the bullshit, Dad's church, found the Navy, then that trouble down in Norfolk, and another night, so fucking stoned, woke up with the big sun on my shoulder, nothing to be frightened of.

Even though the words spilled out of control, as if the dam had burst, she could tell he wasn't telling her everything—from the way he drew circles on the counter with his fingers, and chuffed air out of his nose, and looked past her toward the street.

"So we're okay?" he asked when he was done. He finally looked into her eyes. He took her hand.

She nodded. Tina wondered if her dad would like Ben, tattoos and all.

Tina leaned against the truck and let Ben grope. She couldn't see him, but she could feel his callused fingers, playing her, and she could smell him: coffee and cigarettes, the beer.

"If you want out so bad, why don't you just leave?" Her breath came in short bursts at his probing touch, at the scrape of his tongue on her neck. She didn't want him to leave. Or she did. They'd go together. "How can they stop you?"

"Why don't *you* leave? You've got those big plans. What's holding you back?"

"It's not that simple," Tina said. There was her mom, for one thing. Her dad.

"Bingo," Ben said. He kissed her again, slipping his tongue inside, working his fingers, grinding against her. "And besides, I told you. I found what I was looking for."

The heat of the pickup soaked into her while she fumbled with Ben's belt. His mouth and hands were everywhere and that was okay, more than okay in fact; she didn't want to talk about church anymore, or parents, or what was holding her back, especially not about holding back. He rubbed against her and bit her ear and rubbed some more. He shimmied her jeans over her hips, she yanked at his zipper, he clawed at her panties, she pulled him free.

And then he groaned. His weight went dead, pinning her against the truck. He backed into the dark and disappeared.

"Hey! Don't leave me here!" She zipped up, throbbing and damp.

She heard footsteps, and then he was back by her side, leaning on the fender. He lit a cigarette, gave her one, and they smoked. He went to the bed of the Ford and returned with a backpack and flashlight. He shined it in her eyes. She thought he was going to say something about what had just happened, and she'd have to be the one to give comfort. And she would happily give it, but he kept his mouth shut, as though she wasn't supposed to know. He took her hand and pulled her into the woods. She hesitated, but he tightened his grip and yanked.

She figured they were headed to a cabin. The church thing was surely a joke. He said she'd enjoy it, and there wasn't much she'd enjoy more than getting into bed in a cozy mountain cabin, maybe with a crackling fire, and giving him another chance. He wouldn't be in such a rush this time. They could talk about what bothered him. They could make plans about going away.

Ben moved faster and dragged her to her feet when she stumbled.

The uphill trail was clean—no rocks, no tree limbs, the dirt packed smooth—and with the help of Ben's flashlight they moved quickly through the switchbacks. Ben took a bottle of water out of the pack and offered it to Tina. She drank and then he drank. There was no cabin in sight, but she was afraid to ask again where they were going. Men didn't like so many questions, did they? It would be better to turn back, hurry down to the truck, and lock herself inside until daylight. He handed her the bottle and she drank again; he licked a trickle off her chin. Their wet mouths kissed. He stroked her face. He took her hand, gentler now, and they hiked on.

Ben shined the flashlight on a boulder twice his height, then on a staircase of smaller stones. She followed him up the steps. Her foot slipped on a loose rock, but Ben stopped her fall. Finally they stood on the flat, smooth surface of the boulder, gazing out at the dark hills below. Tina shivered in the breeze and Ben wrapped an arm around her. They sat.

"Our throne," Ben said and chuckled. He pointed to tiny white lights in the distance, scattered farmhouses. Red lights moved away on a highway, down the slope. Ben aimed the beam to his left, on the trees towering over them, their branches fluttering and spread, as if ready for flight. He switched it off, pulling the blackness over them again, and lay back on the rock slab.

Okay, thought Tina. We're sitting on a giant rock, on top of a mountain, he's got a girl who desperately wants to party, and what— he's taking a nap? She was cold, she had to pee, and if sex wasn't on the menu she wouldn't turn down pizza and a beer, or even a granola bar if Ben had one in that pack of his. A cigarette would be good, too. Ben tugged her shirt, lightly, and pulled her down next to him. She laid her head on his shoulder and cuddled under his arm.

Next thing she knew, Ben was nudging her awake. The sky was shades of gray, lighter in the distance. There had been only a few scattered lights before, like lost stars, but now she could make out rolling hills, a dilapidated barn, a black lake. The twitter and cackle of birds came from everywhere, above and below, call and response.

Ben stood, spread his arms and held them there. She gazed up at him from her spot on the rock. He looked so tall, a pale totem pole. A white cross. His t-shirt fluttered in the breeze. He hummed—a deep, droning buzz. Ben pulled the Java Mountain t-shirt over his head and let it fall. The wordless hum changed pitch, higher, and now Tina could hear it all around her. She got to her feet, stiff from sleeping on the rock, and hugged herself against the chill.

"Aren't you cold?" she asked. "And what the hell is that noise?"

The breeze picked up and she stepped behind him. The blue sun seemed to glow on his back. She hesitated, then touched the mark in the center, spiraling her red nail in wider and wider circles. Ben hummed louder, tilting his head upward. Tina moved in close, put her arms around him, hands on his flat belly, and rested her cheek on the sun.

She slipped her fingers inside Ben's jeans. "Can we go now?"

The chant grew louder still. Yellow rays peeked over the hills into the red sky. Tina's hands moved lower, deep down. He dropped his arms and pulled free.

Tina didn't understand. She was giving Ben a chance to redeem himself, to prove he was meant for her. She was offering herself. She should climb off the boulder right now, she should kiss this asshole goodbye, and head back to town.

The hum rose again, from all directions.

She spun around to look for the source of the hum and gasped when she saw an older man down in the grass below the boulder, also shirtless, with his flabby arms spread just like Ben's, a dark patch on his back—the same giant blue sun. He looked familiar, someone she'd seen in town, or in school. Now she saw three other men at the edge of the woods, all facing the rising sun. They had the mark on their backs, too. Dab's father, maybe, the owner of the antique shop, a customer from the Bazaar. She spun again. A cluster of bare-chested men stood on the hillside above and behind her, arms spread, humming, faces beaming in the new light.

"Who are you people?" The men kept their eyes on the sun. "What the fuck is this?" No one answered. "Are you all nuts?" She moved toward the stairs. "I'm going now, Ben."

Ben gripped her am. "I thought you'd understand. After everything you said. This is the answer."

"You're hurting me." Tina pried his fingers loose, but he held her fast in his arms. "I want to go, Ben. Can't we please go?"

"But the sun's not up yet." Ben turned back to the sun, now just winking above the horizon. "The sun is our true father. The savage source."

"This is creepy, Ben. Let me go." She writhed in his grasp. "We could go away. The two of us. We could get out of this dump. We don't need these wackos. We could be together."

"We're helpless without him. We owe everything to him. We seek his blessing." Ben hummed and inched toward the boulder's edge, pulling Tina with him. "Don't you see? Mithra is the true creator." They stood on the precipice.

Ben pinned Tina's arms to her sides.

"What are you doing?"

His grasp tightened.

"We could go back to my place. We'd be good together, you and me." Tina's panicked eyes darted from tree to meadow to windy lake. Dozens of men, all with the scorching tattoo on their backs, stepped in the direction of the sun, arms raised, paying no attention to her. The drone had become a hymn, words she couldn't make out, louder and louder. A gray-bearded man, with a leafy crown on his head, led the way. Tina recognized Mr. Rush, Pam's father. Following him was Mr. Montgomery, the high school basketball coach.

The breeze carried the scent of pine. The sky was yellow now, the sun a wedge glinting off the lake.

She struggled in Ben's arms. Who were these men? What were they going to do to her?

"What are you afraid of, Tina? I just want you to see the truth." Tina kicked at Ben's legs. "Look at the sun. Be still, and look."

Half the sun was above the horizon.

"Please," Tina said softly, so the other men wouldn't hear. "I'll do anything you want. Just let me go." She made a last attempt to break free, and his long, thin arms unfolded, letting her go. She ran to the steps.

"*Sol Invicto Comiti*," Ben chanted, his voice one with the others. The hills choired among themselves. He hovered near the edge of the boulder. "*Sol Invicto Comiti*."

Tina started down the steps.

"*Sol Invicto Comiti*."

She turned to watch and knelt on the cold stone.

"*Sol Invicto Comiti*." Ben faced the sun and spread his arms wide as he chanted.

The sun loomed nearly full, the chant even louder now, and Tina saw the half-naked men converging on the boulder. Mr. McQuain from the pharmacy. And was that Dwight, the bartender at Rocky's?

"*Sol Invicto Comiti*."

The chant was right below Tina, the sun in her eyes, her knees scraping the rock.

"Ben," Tina said softly. She listened to the voices of the men, heard the music of celebration and devotion. She'd never heard anything like it.

"Mithra gives us strength," Ben sang. He raised his arms higher still.

"Please, Ben," she said, although she was no longer sure what he could give her. She rose and joined him on the edge, shivering. The dancing flames on his back were beautiful and glowing in the raw light. She wrapped her arms around him and rested her cheek on his shoulder. Warmth returned to her face, her body.

"*Sol Invicto Comiti*."

A hawk circled lazily overhead. A bobwhite whistled in the trees. Below, and on the hillside above, the men stood erect, facing east, as the sun jumped free of the horizon.

THE CLATTERING OF BONES

Walt didn't feel like going out. It wasn't the first time, and Patsy got that look on her face, clenched and squinty, as if everything was his fault—the July heat, the near-dry well, even the rat snake that had coiled on the driveway one sunny afternoon. She jerked her purse off the counter and dug for a cigarette, even though she'd sworn to quit. She stood there, puffing angry clouds at him like smoke signals.

"Damned if I'm going to sit around all night watching TV," she'd said. Only it was more of a growl, the way it came out in a deep, wet voice, at the back of her throat.

"Suit yourself," Walt said. Walt had the news on—a drought update had caught his eye—and Patsy traipsed back and forth from bedroom to kitchen, he guessed so he'd see her progress in getting ready to go without him. First it was the hair. She fixed it up high, as she did when they used to go dancing—back when Walt worked at the lumberyard and they liked to party, had big plans for the future, kids, trips to Opryland. She came out in her panties and bra, not the low-cut, flesh-colored thing she wore sometimes with a blouse half-unbuttoned, but a white one that pushed her up and made her look bustier than she really was. She splashed whiskey over ice, stirred in a little 7-Up, and took it into the bedroom. Then she came back in the slinky blue dress Walt gave her two Christmases ago, and the pink coral necklace he bought for a birthday years back, that she gushed over at the time and hardly put on anymore.

The hair had already come undone a little and a long strand dangled off her neck. She shot a look at Walt and went back in the bedroom when she'd freshened up her drink. Next time out her lips were fierce red—clashed with the necklace, Walt thought, but of course he wasn't going to say anything—and she'd added green eye shadow. He'd told her once she looked like a banker's fancy girl with her eyes done up like that, not the wife of a dirt-poor landscaper who couldn't get the topsoil out from under his nails. Patsy took a last gulp of her highball and tossed the ice in the sink, grabbed the keys to the pickup and let the screen door slam behind her.

It was after dawn when the Ford pulled in and skidded on the gravel to about an inch from a load of stone Walt planned to lay in Miz Doak's garden. He watched out the bedroom window, saw the whole thing, how Patsy stumbled getting down from the cab and sneaked a look around, as if she was afraid the McKennas across the road would see. He didn't want her to see him either, so he slid back in bed, although it wasn't as if he'd slept at all. Not worried about her exactly, since she'd done it before, but wondering if maybe this time she wasn't coming back.

Her hair was completely down by then. She rattled the necklace onto the bureau, like she was rolling dice. She kicked off the spike heels, let the dress crumple to the floor and fell into bed without once looking at Walt. Didn't care that he saw, he guessed, or didn't want to know.

The next night, without a word passing between them, Walt moved to the sofa—a frilly, flowered number he'd never liked but had learned to put up with, grown lumpy and bowed in the decade he and Patsy had been married. He was still there a week later, but giving some thought to what he could do to make things right between them. It couldn't go on that way forever.

On Sunday, as if a midsummer morning didn't come early enough as it was, down the road Miz Doak's rooster started hollering at first light and a chorus of her woeful cows chimed in. Patsy'd wake up mean, Walt knew, coming in late again, after three. He swung his legs off the sofa, folded the sheets, piled the board-thin pillow on top, smoothed the yellowed case. Now the mule started to bray and there was another voice in the mix, high-pitched, like a whinny. But Walt knew Miz Doak's last mare was a year dead, and the only other horses in the hollow were another mile upcountry.

Walt shuffled across the gritty kitchen floor and switched on the light over the stove. Toss yesterday's grounds in the compost bin, rinse the pot, one scoop, two . . . six, pour in the water, filtered, not from the tap, Patsy hates the taste of the well water. "Like chalk and tin cans in my mouth at the same time," she says, when he forgets. He cinched his old plaid robe tighter, though the day was already warm, and leaned against the sink to peer into the yard, see what the weather had to offer. High clouds. No rain in sight, no relief. The coffee maker crackled, and dribbled into the pot. Something moved out back.

Ducking down, to see under the redbuds and past the gangly walnut that presided over the backyard like an archdeacon, Walt noticed the gassy smell in the drain—cabbage from his own garden, foul when left to rot like that. Not from last night—last night they'd skipped supper—but from the night before. The coffee maker still popped and dripped. There, he saw it again. Something definitely moved.

Through the leaves, he could just make out the muzzle nodding, inches off the ground, as if the deer wanted to graze. Odd to see a deer so close to the house, in full light. At dawn maybe, in twilight safety, but the sun had been up a good hour. Walt yanked the pot off the burner and let coffee drizzle into a mug, then slipped the pot back. He almost turned to see if Patsy'd witnessed the maneuver. "Walter, don't do that," she'd say. "It makes a mess. Can't you wait?" It was funny when she was the one complaining about a mess. Talk about the pot . . . Walt took his cup to the dining room, to get a better view of the fence.

Dining room. That was a joke, too. More like a wide spot in the living room where the hand-me-down table had landed last year when they moved in. The house had seemed just right at the time, with room for the coming baby, and a sunlit yard for Walt's garden.

But Patsy's miscarriage derailed the unpacking—unopened boxes were still stacked in a corner of the bedroom and the dank basement—and they'd never figured out what to do with the table, short of Patsy's idea of chucking it in the fireplace. Walt pulled a chair close to the window.

The glass was streaked and dull. But there was the deer, half in the yard, half out, slung over the barbed wire fence like a musty blanket on a clothesline. Walt opened the window, and instantly regretted it. The doe had seen him, or heard the grating of the warped frame; she struggled and kicked, craned her neck. Her front hooves pounded the dirt and raised a dust storm. The wire shuddered. Blood trickled down the inside of her hindquarters, a leg twisted between strands, snagged on a barb. Walt backed away from the window. She's killing herself, he thought. Got to keep her calm. Only way to save her.

Patsy was in the kitchen now, leaning against the stove. She lifted her coffee cup with two hands and eyed Walt as he bent over the sink.

"What the hell are you doing?"

"There's a deer. On the fence. Trying to figure out what I can do to help her."

"If you had a gun, like every other man in this county, you'd know what to do." She looked over his shoulder. "Can't see anything," she said.

"Not the season, honey, even if—"

"But you'd let it die slow?"

"Not if I can help it."

Walt left Patsy inside and peeked around the corner of the house, but the deer saw him and started thrashing again, slashing a trough with her hooves, kicking her hind legs out, stretching her neck up to make herself look bigger. He'd seen dogs do that, to fool larger animals. If he could keep her quiet, maybe cut the wire or find a way to lift her off the fence, she might have a chance. The closer he got, the harder she struggled, and that's when he thought of the jute sacks. Sometimes Patsy bought a forty-pound bag of potatoes from the wholesale market and Walt saved them.

"They're filthy," Patsy'd crabbed when he rescued the first one from the trash. "They'll just be more clutter." To Walt it didn't seem much different from hording plastic tubs for leftovers, or grocery bags for the garbage, but Patsy wouldn't listen.

"I'll find a use for 'em," he'd said.

They were in the garage, under a stack of bricks left over from when he'd redone the front walk. That was in the fall, when Patsy'd been so snappish and distant he couldn't stand to be around her, and he'd invented time-eating projects in the yard—the walkway, transplanting the azaleas, setting out dozens of bulbs and daylilies. Those extra bricks he piled beside the crib he'd painted for the baby, tucked behind boxes so Patsy wouldn't have to see it.

He came out the side door so as not to spook the doe. He'd have to work fast, run hard to where she was, grab her neck to keep her still, and slip that sack over her head. Then she'd settle down, blinded, and in a minute she'd be calm enough for him to take the next step. Except now he saw his cutters would be no match for the heavy-gauge wire. And he wasn't sure how he was going to lift her off that top rung without hurting her even worse, especially with her hind legs caught up in the next two strands.

But there was no sneaking up on her; the doe wouldn't let him near. Walt held the putrid bag open like a butterfly net, but when he came close her flailing grew so wild he could hear the barbs rip through her flesh and the fur actually flew. He'd always thought that was a dumb expression, but there was no denying the hair on the doe's hide floated in the air like dandelion fluff. This is killing her, Walt thought, and backed off.

He poured more coffee and watched from the dining room window. The deer's struggle slowed, but every now and then she'd lift her head or twitch her ears and he knew she was still alive. There weren't many options left. He could call a neighbor—John Craig down the road was a good man—and maybe the two of them could get the deer down, even with all her crazy dancing. Maybe she was going to be still now, maybe she'd figure out he only wanted to help.

Or he could call the Sheriff. Walt wasn't on particularly good terms with the Sheriff's office, didn't like their coming around all the time, like this spring when one of his oh-so-helpful neighbors had called to report an incident at Walt and Patsy's place. It had all been a misunderstanding—Patsy'd screamed bloody murder when she saw the garden shears in his hands, probably remembering another incident, ancient history, when he'd just been laid off and they were both drunk, involving a butcher knife and shouted threats. And there'd been that muddle in high school, not so long ago really: pranks with beer cans and spray paint, brawls with boys from Defiance, getting high and racing down country roads. It got so the Sheriff came looking for Walt and his buddies at the first sign of mischief.

All behind him now. It wasn't as hard to quit drinking as he'd thought it would be, and Patsy went right along with him, even seemed relieved. It was part of their plan, and things were good for a while, peaceful, although they'd had to get by on Patsy's tips from the nail salon while he hunted for work. And when Walt got hired on as a landscaper, life seemed downright sunny; they saved a little money, Patsy got pregnant, and they bought the house. But the Sheriff still stopped by from time to time, as if he figured Walt was destined for trouble.

So Walt didn't want the Sheriff's help. He made some calls. The Game Department was no good, when he finally got through to somebody. She was polite enough, but said there was nothing they could do, and suggested he call Transportation. That made no sense to him but he called and, it being Sunday, got no answer anyway. It dawned on him they'd be the folks to clear away road kill, and then he wished he hadn't left his name on their answering machine. That wasn't what he wanted at all. The Wildlife Center didn't do rescues in the field. "You ought to call the Sheriff," they said.

Walt set his coffee cup on the dining table, noticed the dust fly and brushed his hand across the surface, leaving stripes that turned his fingers gray. He waited.

Patsy made herself breakfast—Walt heard butter sizzling in the skillet and then the crack of eggs and Patsy's humming as she stood over the stove with a spatula, the ting as the bread landed in the toaster. Walt drank his coffee, kept an eye on the doe.

He turned when he heard the click of Patsy's heels on the linoleum. She stood in the doorway, a plate in one open hand like a serving tray, sopping up runny yoke with her toast.

"You going to watch that damn deer all day?" Patsy's nails, freshly lacquered in a shade of pink that brought undercooked pork to Walt's mind, scraped the underside of the plate. "That thing better be gone by the time I get back." She was going to church with her sister, Molly, then a movie at the mall and shopping afterward—a high school ritual they hadn't grown out of. Patsy's plate rattled in the sink, just as Molly honked out front. The screen door slammed and Walt didn't have to get up to picture the two women gunning away in Molly's beat-up Grand Am, hair fluttering out the windows, trailing the oldies station behind them like exhaust. Beat-up because it wasn't hers and she didn't give a damn what her ex-boyfriend, Darryl, had to say if he ever showed up to claim it. Probably wasn't worth it to him, knowing he'd have to get past her first.

Now Walt made something to eat. He and Patsy hardly ever ate breakfast together anymore, and she'd stopped cooking for him months ago. Sometimes he fixed supper, but Patsy didn't show much interest and most of the food went into the trash, or down the drain. While he waited for his toast, he watched the deer for signs of life. It was still, maybe the head bobbed, but Walt wasn't sure. He found the butter and jam and returned to his spot by the window, feeling like he was at the movies, too. He watched a rabbit nibble on the spirea he'd just planted, then bolt into the woods with another rabbit in pursuit. He finished the toast, catching the crumbs in his cupped palm, and licked the jam off his fingers. A flashy cardinal landed on the feeder to peck at the sunflower seeds and then was joined by his drab mate. Walt tapped on the window and the birds scudded into the sycamore at the edge of the yard.

That sent the deer into a paroxysm that startled Walt. The front legs stirred up even more dirt and that white tail flew, her head high, as if she were just now starting her jump over the fence, and dropped fast when she came up short. The hind legs banged against the barbed wire and he could hear the twang even inside the house. And then she was still.

He didn't blink for fear of missing any twitch of movement. But there was nothing. The hooves were planted, motionless. The wires settled. The neck hung, snout drooping close to the ground. The eyes stared. The rabbits ran back into sight. The birds forgot about him and returned to feed.

Now he had a different problem, but at least he knew what to do. There was no hurry. Walt showered and dressed, ready for chores. He had a fallen tree to clear down by the creek, and the garden needed attention. He'd let the grass get higher than he should; it would be sluggish mowing.

He took a break around three. Careful to slip off his boots before he traipsed dirt into the house, Walt filled a glass with ice and poured warm Coke. He felt cooler already, just listening to the ice crackle and feeling the Coke spit on his hand. He peeled off his sweaty t-shirt and traded it for a dry one, held the glass to his forehead, ducked down again to see the deer. Still dead, he thought, and shook his head. Not funny, not . . . respectful. The cold Coke burned his throat, hammered his head just behind his eyes.

Out back now, the deed couldn't be avoided any longer. He took a few steps toward the deer and stopped. Took a few more. Flies hummed in a chorus like they enjoyed their work, swarming on the doe's eyes, the nostrils, the trail of blood on her legs. He took a few more steps and the swarm lifted and settled again, and he wondered if all those thousands of flies had gone back to their own spot on the carcass or if maybe they'd taken that opportunity to change places. Now the stench was noticeable. The doe had been straddled there for hours in the sun, baking, rotting, and it didn't take long for the smell to start. But he was close enough to see what he needed to see. She'd managed to get a hind leg over one wire and twisted under the next, and it was squeezed around her like a paper clip; barbs had sliced through the hide in a couple of places, and he could almost picture the wire sawing her in half.

A saw. He might need a saw, but didn't relish having to cut through bone just to get the deer off the damn fence.

In the garage, he settled on the tools for the job: gloves, a hoe, a trowel in case the hoe didn't work. The flies buzzed off when he came back, sounding angry, mad to get to their prize. Holding his breath and gripping the deer's front legs, he lifted. Heavier than he'd expected, and he couldn't do it—she didn't look that big with her head down—and they were on an incline so lifting from the front was moving her uphill, the lift harder. But the leg was stuck in the wires anyway, and just lifting wouldn't have done the trick. He tried to pry the leg loose with the hoe, but that was no good. With his boot he jammed the lower wire down and pulled up with his hand, finally managed to untwist that leg and let it spring free. Then he vaulted the fence and came at her from behind. He wasn't holding his breath anymore, just working fast to get it over with. The smell was bad, but the flies were worse. It seemed like they were after *his* eyes, *his* nostrils now. He tried to shoo them away, but there were too damn many.

One, two, three, lift, and she was off the fence, on the ground, neck twisted and ugly like a train wreck, open black eyes unforgiving. Her brown hair coated the top wire where the body had creased, and blood in the dust darkened and seeped into the rocky soil. Walt crouched, grabbed the hind legs just above the hooves, and pulled the doe under the fence. He dragged her through the tall weeds, the thistle and wild roses, apologized for the thorns that added insult to injury. The abandoned pasture parted, and they left a trail of crushed grass and shivering Queen Anne's lace. He pulled, his breath coming hard as he tugged the weight uphill, not from the exertion so much, but just the sadness of what he had to do. The dry soil crumbled under his boots; sweat boiled out of him. He stopped. Dropped the legs. The flies swarmed to the body. Walt turned his head and backed away.

He set the tools on their pegs in the garage, hung the bloodstained gloves above the bench, next to the pliers and the useless wire cutters, and went inside. No sign of Patsy yet. He washed up, drank another Coke, eyed Patsy's bottle of whiskey, lay on the sofa.

***

First one, circling high, gliding like a kid's kite until it sees the doe on the hillside, or smells her, swoops down for a clumsy landing, waddles over, hunched wings nearly hiding the small poppy skull, and pecks at the deer, rips away a bit of hide with the black hook of its beak. Then it launches and soars, drifts over the hillside and disappears. Later, letting the flesh melt in the sun, the vulture comes back with another, and a few more follow, and then the sky is full of them, wafting toward the doe. One lands and makes for the carrion, then another. A pair roosts in the walnut tree, peering down, waiting their turn. Then the ground is covered with the birds, wrestling over the corpse, stripping meat from the skeleton, spreading their wings in mutual reproach. They'll be silent, for the most part, a whine or a hiss to stake a claim, but the sounds are the ripping and tearing of the hide and flesh, the clattering of bones. It'll take a day, maybe two, to pick her clean.

The sun dropped behind the pines on Bald Rock Hill, spilled pinks and oranges over the ridge, left the sky violet black. Walt sat on the porch, watched the swallows until they became invisible, swatted at the mosquitoes, listened for the growl of Molly's Grand Am. Darryl's Grand Am. Nothing. He gave it another hour.

Inside he found a backpack he used sometimes, on hikes up in the Blue Ridge, or when he was out in the field on long summer days. When he picked it up he knew it still had a water bottle from the last trip. Loose change clinked in the side pocket. It wouldn't hold much, but it wouldn't need to. He pulled briefs out of the bureau, socks, a few t-shirts, just enough to get by for a few days, a week. He'd get the rest later, after he found a place. He went out to the garage. He ran his hand over the glossy white of the crib, the pink and blue trim, traced the stenciled flowers with his finger. Then he tossed the pack into the truck bed, next to his toolbox and a pair of muddy boots, and climbed in.

Gravel spun under the tires, headlights washed over the vacant fence, and Walt pulled the Ford onto the dark road.

HAND-PAINTED ANGEL

Remember Bosco?" my brother asks. It's Christmas Eve morning and we're in Dad's kitchen, both of us early risers. I'm making coffee, and Tim is gazing out the window watching Dad start his chores in the purple dawn, feeding the animals, chopping firewood. My wife, Emily, is asleep upstairs.

"Of course I remember. He was a great dog." Bosco was our chocolate Lab when we were kids. I remember Dad phoning when I was in school down in Blacksburg, his voice as choked up as it ever got, to tell me he how he'd been with the old boy, whispering to him and stroking his head, when the vet put him to sleep. I know Tim is thinking of Bosco because Bosco's successor, Baron, a mutt from the shelter, is limping along behind the old man, trying to keep up, and we know how attached Dad is. It'll be even harder this time.

The coffee maker is gurgling, and the smell makes me hungry. I find the bacon and eggs we picked up at the Food Lion on our way into town yesterday, pull out the skillet, and light the stove. Emily loves coming to the farm. She says it brings out my domestic side, which she doesn't get to see at home. We've been together five years, since our last year of law school, married for three. She works just as hard as I do, but that's about to change, or at least the focus of her attention will. She's pregnant. We told her folks on the phone last week, because she couldn't keep a secret like that from her mother, but we haven't told anyone else. Dad is going to love being a Grandpa, and Timmy will be a terrific uncle.

I hear the shower so I know the coffee got Emily moving. Dad is stomping his feet on the back porch, shaking off the light snow we had in the night.

"Are you going to tell him?" I ask my brother. Tim is a year younger, and we're tight. We shared an apartment in college, he helped me pull myself together when I was partying a lot back then, and he was best man at our wedding. He and Emily get along great and he drives down from D.C. to visit us in Richmond probably once a month. He came out to us a couple of years ago, although he knew we already knew. I stopped trying to fix him up with Emily's sorority sisters a long time back when I figured it out, although we didn't talk about it at the time. It doesn't matter. I love him. We love him.

"I don't think I can, Teddy." Tim does fundraising for a non-profit and has just moved in with his boyfriend, Gareth, a medical student from South Africa, to an apartment in Dupont Circle. Emily and I like Gareth, and find his lilting accent charming. We know Tim considered bringing Gareth along on this visit, but chickened out at the last minute, so Gareth will spend Christmas alone in the city. Tim says he understands.

Dad and Baron are inside now, and Baron heads directly for his spot by the stove. It's a floor of soft, broad pine planks, and his spot is worn smooth. I try to remember if that was Bosco's spot, too, and I think it was. Dad pours himself a cup of coffee and stands next to Tim, both of them looking outside. The sky is lighter now, just a little pink left.

Emily comes in wearing my old plaid robe and her own fuzzy slippers. The robe isn't the only thing we found in my old bedroom closet—high school letter jacket, baseball bat and glove, various other sports paraphernalia. I think Mom had planned to send my old clothes to Goodwill, maybe turn it into a sewing room, but when she passed away Dad left everything alone, as if he couldn't bear to lose one more part of the family, even if it was cast-off, outgrown crap. But that robe looks great on Emily. She pats Baron on the head, kisses Tim and Dad, then comes and puts her arms around me. She smells like the minty soap my Dad has in the bathroom, the same brand Mom always bought.

The bacon is popping and just about ready; Emily sets the table. She talks about what we're all doing today: the men—she calls us "the men" as if she weren't the only woman—will head into the woods behind the house to find a tree; she's got cookies to bake and presents to wrap; then we're all heading into Rugglesville in the afternoon to carry on a couple of family traditions. We'll sip mulled cider at the coffee house downtown, then walk along Central Avenue and admire the Christmas decorations, which will be exactly the same as they've always been, and stop in the Bazaar to choose this year's family ornament. Decorating will be tonight, after we've finished off the cold-cut platter—another Callison family tradition—and we'll top the day off with pumpkin pie and whipped cream.

"What would we do without Emily," Dad says, grinning. "We wouldn't know to put one foot in front of the other if she didn't remind us." He winks at me. Tim chuckles while Emily posts her hands on her hips and pretends to be indignant.

"Or which pot to piss in," she says and can't keep from laughing. It's all familiar, all remembered lines from Christmases past.

I open the spice cabinet to get salt and pepper for the eggs and see something that isn't familiar: little amber pill bottles, with Dad's name on the prescription labels—small white tablets in one, big blue ones in the other.

"What's this?" I hold the bottles up for Dad to see.

He squints in my direction. We've told him at various times over the years he needs glasses, but he never listens. He's got these little magnifying glasses he picked up at a grocery store and he uses those to read the paper when he thinks no one is watching. He waves dismissively.

"Oh, that's nothing. Doctor says the blood pressure's a little high. No big deal."

I look at the eggs and bacon I've just heaped onto the serving platter, grease already forming a little vein-clogging pool. I turn to

Tim, whose face registers concern. I don't know much about these things, but he's the one who lives with an almost-doctor.

"You should watch what you eat, though, right?" Tim says.

"An egg now and then ain't gonna kill me," Dad says, pulling out a chair for Emily to sit. He plops down next to her. "Come on. Let's eat. We've got things to do."

After breakfast, "the men" bundle up—it's colder this morning than when we arrived last night—and head for the woods. Baron comes too. You can see in his eyes he thinks he's obligated, even though the kitchen is warm and Emily is a likely soft touch for treats. But he tags along with Dad. Tim and I carry the ax and saw. The first year I was with Emily, she joined the tree-hunting party. She said we needed a woman's eye to pick a good tree. I think she noticed that didn't sit too well with Dad, since Mom wasn't long gone at that point. Mom always stayed behind to bake. Emily's the sort of woman who accepts that times change, but people don't necessarily change along with them. So now she lets "the men" do their thing, and she bakes. It's a small price, she says.

We don't talk much on our expedition, at least not about anything important. Tech has had a good season and they're going to a New Year's Day bowl, so we talk about that for a while. Tim's not a football fan, and Dad is mostly interested because I am. Dad mentions an accident on the Interstate last week that had traffic backed up for ten miles; he thought he was going to have to do his business in the bushes, with or without T.P., but the mess cleared in time. I think Tim might seize a lull in the conversation to tell Dad what he's been trying to tell him for years, "By the way, Dad . . .," but he doesn't do it and the moment passes when Dad comes up with another local tidbit to share, something about a crazy woman who years ago kidnapped her daughter from her ex-husband and finally came back to face the consequences.

Actually, I'm looking for a chance to talk about something, too. Not about the baby. Emily and I plan to tell them the news on Christmas morning, when Dad's sister Irene and her husband Marvin come over and we exchange gifts. I haven't even told Emily this yet because I just found out and I'm not sure how she'll take it. I'm not even sure how I feel about it. The law firm I joined right out of school merged last year with a big national firm, and there's been some shuffling of lawyers to integrate the firm cultures, which is another way of saying they want to erase whatever sense of local identity we had in Richmond. The partner I work for is moving to Los Angeles and he wants me to come, too. It'll mean a lot more money and a fast track to promotion, but L.A. is far away. I want to ask Dad and Tim what they think before I talk to Emily, but I realize they've got their own problems, and maybe now isn't the right time.

We find the tree—Tim and I know from years of experience that we are along to do the cutting and hauling, but Dad does the picking—and drag it down the hill to the house. We shake the dead needles out of it and when we lean it up against the barn Tim reaches in and pulls out a birds' nest. We all laugh about that. Baron barks at the nest.

Inside, the cookies are in the oven, the breakfast dishes are drying in the rack, and the windows are steamy. Emily must be getting dressed for the next item on the agenda.

When we head out again, Baron is content to curl up by the stove. We all sample the cookies. There's no way Baron can get up on the counter to bother them, but Emily pushes them way back against the wall anyway.

The sky has filled with thick clouds, and Emily hopes that means snow. She grew up in Atlanta, and it seems we get mostly ice storms down in Richmond, so heavy snow is still a treat for her. It makes me think how she'll react to the idea of California. We take our new Range Rover into town. Dad only has the pickup these days, and the five of us would be a tight fit in Tim's VW. We have our cider and then walk up one side of Central and down the other. Emily spots an antique store that's new since our last visit and we check it out. Tim lingers near the front, chatting with a slim blond guy and Dad parks in a wing chair for the duration. We don't stay long. Last stop is the Bazaar.

The place is decked out in garlands and wreaths, and there are Christmas carols playing on a radio somewhere. A perky girl with pink hair waves at us when we come in, but doesn't move from the cash register, where she's perched on a stool reading *People* magazine. The ornaments are right up front, as usual, and it doesn't take long for each of us to pick one out. Tim's is pretty normal for him—a gold foil star, with a lacy pattern that makes it look like a snowflake. It's nice, but I happen to think it would be lost on our tree, where we're still hanging construction paper snowmen Tim and I made in elementary school. Emily is drawn to the ceramic pieces and has her hands on one that looks like baby Jesus, but then chooses an ornament in the shape of a dog. I know she thinks Dad will like that. I guess I lack Emily's creativity and Tim's style, and I'm drawn to a plain red ball with a satiny finish. We fully expect Dad to come up with the same ugly egg he always does, with sequins and bows or a glittering American flag, but we're in for a surprise. He's picked up a cone-shaped glass bulb, painted to look like an angel, but somehow the painting is on the inside. There's a gold ribbon for hanging. We each handle it carefully, studying the bulb to figure out how it was made.

"It's Chinese," says the girl with the pink hair. "Hand-painted."

Every year there's an argument about the ornament. It's never serious, of course, but there's supposed to be a debate. A negotiation. "I'll give you two chocolate-covered cherries and a drumstick if you vote for mine," someone might say. "I'll vote for yours next year, if you vote for mine now." It's tradition.

But we're stunned by the hand-painted angel and have nothing to offer.

"I love it," Emily says.

"Me too," Tim says. I just nod.

Dad carries the ornament to the pink-haired girl, who locates a box of just the right length, wraps the angel in tissue, and lays it inside. We head home in the dark.

Baron is happy to see us and even joins Dad for the evening chores. As soon as Dad is outside, Tim goes into the living room. I can hear him talking quietly on the phone to Gareth. Emily goes upstairs to rest for a few minutes, and I'm alone in the kitchen. I think this is a good time to talk to Dad about L.A. I watch him put out feed for his sheep and then lean on the fence with his head down, as if he's catching his breath, or something worse. I grab my coat and am on the porch with a foot on the steps, when he straightens up and whistles for Baron.

"You okay, Dad?" I ask when he's on the porch.

"A little tired," he says.

Tim is at the kitchen table when we come in. Dad pulls three Heinekens out of the refrigerator. This is part of the tradition. We clink bottles and sip. Everything feels right, but just on the verge of a breakdown, like a knot that's about to come untied. We can keep going for now, but this might be the end. That knot's not going to hold forever.

Emily joins us. She's changed sweaters and brushed her hair; she looks great, exactly like the girl I fell in love with, and I have to kiss her. Dad and Tim laugh. At this point in the ritual, Emily should be opening a bottle of wine. We even picked up a nice chardonnay with the groceries—a little subterfuge Emily thought of—but she gets bottled water out of the refrigerator instead. Dad and Tim look at her as she sits at the kitchen table.

"You want me to open the wine?" Dad asks.

"No thanks," she says. Now Dad and Tim look at each other. Emily's breaking tradition.

"Can I tell them?" I ask.

"Might as well," she says. She's got as broad a grin as I've ever seen. We've been looking forward to this moment.

They're both thrilled, as we knew they would be. Emily and I have talked about names already, even though it's early yet. "We're thinking Alice if it's a girl," I say. Alice was my mother's name. Dad sits down when he hears that.

"Or Henry if it's a boy," Emily says. That's my Dad's name— Hank.

We fix the traditional cold-cut and relish tray—everyone has a favorite. Dad likes salami and provolone cheese and he'll basically just make a sandwich out of it, even though we tell him, all of us at once, that those aren't the best choices for his condition. Tim insists on bologna. He says it's in honor of Mom and the daily bologna and American cheese sandwiches when we were kids. I like thick slices of ham, and Emily always wants turkey, despite the whole roast bird we'll have tomorrow. Given the way the ornament shopping went, maybe we would have been able to agree on one thing for Christmas Eve supper this year, like smoked salmon or something, but anyway we all get what we want.

It's tree-trimming time. I know families who put up their tree just after Thanksgiving and leave it up until New Year's or later. Not us. Up on Christmas Eve and down it comes as soon as the holiday is over. Dad lets it dry then and uses it for kindling, so it's not really as wasteful as it sounds. Here's what we do. We all open another beer, except Emily, but she's got her water, and bicker good-naturedly about the decorations. "The lights are too bunched," Tim says; "Let's lose the construction paper snowmen," Emily proposes; "Whose idea was tinsel, anyway," I say.

"It's perfect," Dad says.

In the trimming process, we've all reserved the center of the tree, the spot facing the middle of the living room, for the year's family ornament. It was Dad's pick, so he gets the honor of hanging the hand-painted angel. He lifts the ribbon over a small branch and the ornament sways for a moment—Emily gasps because she thinks it's falling—and then hangs straight. Tim turns on the tree lights, and I hit the wall switch at the same time, plunging the rest of the room into darkness. We step away from the tree and admire our work. Dad puts one arm around Tim and one around me. I've already got my arm around Emily. The tree really is perfect.

We bring our pie and whipped cream into the living room, something Mom never would have allowed. Usually we do that part of the ritual in the kitchen, too, but this year we want to be closer to the tree. Baron snoozes at Dad's feet.

In the morning there's a foot of snow on the ground. It's going to make getting back to Richmond tough, but they should have the roads cleared by the next day, when we have to leave. Aunt Irene calls and says they've decided to stay home. I talk to her for a while, then Tim, then Emily is the one to give the news about little Alice or Henry.

There's a coffeecake Emily made, and we slog through the presents. It isn't quite the orgy it was when Tim and I were kids, but there's a lot. Both Tim and I got rawhide bones for Baron. We laugh and Baron doesn't know which one to chew first. Tim gives me a sweater, and I give him a sweater. Dad bought Emily a robe, almost exactly like my old robe, and we laugh about that. Emily and I give Dad a battery-powered drill, something he's wanted for a long time.

Dad looks tired. Tim and I take care of the chores for him—the animals have to be fed, snow or not, and there's wood to be chopped and carried. Emily tends to dinner. The day is quiet, as if we're all under the same thick blanket.

Finally we sit down to dinner.

"Bless us, Oh Lord, for the gifts we are about to receive," intones Dad. We talk about nothing—the sweaters we got, poor Baron's confusion of riches, the pink-haired girl at the Bazaar.

"That hand-painted angel is something," Dad says.

Tim clears his throat. "Dad," he says.

Emily takes my hand under the table.

"I've got something to tell you."

Dad's got a mouthful of turkey and it's almost like Tim planned it that way, so Dad couldn't interrupt.

"I'm gay," Tim says.

Dad looks at Tim, finishes chewing, takes a swallow of beer. He looks at me and Emily, then at Tim.

"And you think I don't know?" he asks.

It's a funny moment. Tim looks at Dad, and Dad looks at Tim. Then he looks at me and points at Tim, shrugs and takes another bite of turkey. Emily laughs, so I laugh, and Tim has no choice but to laugh. Even Baron looks up from his spot by the stove to see what's going on.

So everyone's secret is out but mine, and I'm having too good a time to bring it up. And I realize the reason I haven't said anything is that it isn't for me. I don't want to move to L.A. I'm not even sure I want to stay down in Richmond. I wonder, instead, if the town of Rugglesville, Virginia needs another lawyer, and what Emily and little Alice or Hank might think of moving home.

IN AN UNCHARTED COUNTRY

W alt pulls away from the house in first gear, the pickup whining and slow on the gravel road, because he's not sure he's doing right. Patsy might need him when she gets back from town, she hasn't been herself, won't ever be able to put out of her mind what could have been—if she hadn't lost the baby. But it's been months, months of bitter silence, when for days not a word would pass between them, and he's tried to understand, and he's tired of trying. He shifts up, and the truck gains speed.

"I want you to see someone," Walt had said that afternoon. The drinking had started right away, after she was up and around again— jug wine from the grocery at first, progressing to bourbon supplied by her sister, Molly.

"That new mechanic at Wilson's Garage is kind of cute. How 'bout him?" She swirled the ice in her glass. The sweet charcoal filled his head, settling on his tongue.

"I meant—"

Patsy tossed her drink in Walt's face, the ice cubes tumbling to the linoleum, the cold, peaty booze dripping from his chin.

"I know what you meant," she'd said.

Headlights come fast around the bend by Miz Doak's barn, high beams, and he steers right in case the fool driver doesn't see in time. A familiar Grand Am shoots past, and he hears laughter, but he doesn't think Patsy sees him. Molly's driving, though, so it's hard to tell. They don't slow down.

It's not too late. He could change his mind and turn back, make sure everything's okay. Put coffee on and see that Molly's safe to drive home. "You girls been gone a long time," he'd say, letting the earlier argument slide, trying not to sound like he was accusing her of anything, and Patsy'd unpin her hair and say, "Off to see your girlfriend were you?" and he'd stuff his hands in his pockets and say, "You know it's not like that," and she'd say, "It sure as hell better not be." That's about how it would be. So Walt keeps going.

It's not as if he has any place to go *to*, though. Even though this trouble has been brewing for weeks, he hadn't thought ahead, just threw jeans and a couple of work shirts in the truck when it hit him they weren't ever going to be like they once were. She wasn't and he wasn't, and together they weren't. It was a good run, since they were kids exploring new territory together, the hungry fit of their untested bodies, shared new vistas of grass-altered states. Now he thinks it's better this way, on his own for the first time. She hates the country, always has, and now she can move into town. And he might look for work down in Richmond, not that the city holds any interest for him, but he could do with better pay, a job with a future, a new world.

He thinks about heading over to his brother's place, in the western part of the county. Anthony'd take him in, chalk the fight up to Walt's history of trouble, from high school brawls and drug busts right on down the line, and Ruth probably wouldn't start agitating for him to leave for a couple of days. It would give him time to think.

But he wants to be at the job site early tomorrow, and by the time he gets out west and finds Anthony's new house in the dark and explains everything, it'll be late. Too late.

So he heads into town instead, without a plan. And he laughs, because that's always been the problem. For both of them. Quick to marry after school and then scramble for dead-end jobs, too much booze, a greedy taste for whatever else was available, they go on that way without ever thinking there could be more to life, and then, boom, there's a baby on the way. Time to grow up, make peace with the world, make a plan, get sober. And it worked, for a while, until one day it was over: no baby, no future, no peace.

It's Sunday night and the streets are quiet. There's another pickup and a Camaro parked in front of Rocky's Tavern and he pulls up behind them, lets the motor run while he weighs his options. It's been almost a year for him, but right now he would really like a beer. When Patsy had the miscarriage it was all he could do to hold on, like he was climbing a mountain, clinging to the rocks with one sweaty hand and watching her, finger by finger, slip from his grasp. He wonders if this is where Patsy's been all day, Patsy and Molly. If he goes inside, will they look at him funny, whisper about his cheating wife? She might be, for all he knows, might've been with someone besides Molly these nights she claimed they were out together. Could be he'd see the bastard if he went inside the bar right now.

Or Beth-Ann might be tending bar tonight. Patsy has a notion that Walt's been sleeping with Beth-Ann, just because the girl has big tits and smiled at him once. Maybe he should go in and see Beth-Ann, turn the tables.

Walt bites his lip, something Don, who hired him because he promised to stay sober, told him was sure-fire, said he knew from experience. Walt tastes blood.

He drives away from Rocky's, his hands trembling as if he's cold even though it's dead summer, but the farther away he gets the less he shakes. Still, he coaxes a last salty drop from his lip, savors it on his tongue. He realizes he's come to Schoolhouse Park, near the baseball diamond, the storied scene of high-school antics, and stops there. The place is supposed to be closed, no parking overnight, but the worst that can happen is the cops will tell him to move on and jot another black mark next to his name.

He sleeps fitfully on the front seat, and no one bothers him. In the night, for the first time since he was a boy sharing a room with Anthony, he hears the whistle of a train. They imagined riding the train, making their escape, and Anthony tacked a map to the wall. Walt would close his eyes and throw a dart at the map and they'd plot an adventure in Wyoming, or Maine, or Saskatchewan. The dart once hit Montana, far from any towns or marked roads. "Look at that," Walt had said. "There's nothing there. Big empty space. We'd be the first men to see it, I bet. Uncharted country."

When dawn hits—it's not gradual in town, like it is out at his place—he heads to work. He and Don are starting a new project, landscaping a retirement home, and there won't be much for Walt to do until Don shows up with the new plantings—silver maples along the driveway, dogwoods and crape myrtle in back—and his sketch of where things will go. But he'll do what he can in the meantime, soil prep and whatnot. Don will be pleased.

Don *is* pleased, and the work goes fast despite the drought-hardened dirt. They don't talk much. Are the Red Sox for real? Any rain in the forecast? Walt doesn't tell Don he's left Patsy.

They'll be coming back on Tuesday, the work only half done, so cleanup is light. Walt heads to the Y to shower. Patsy never liked him tracking mud and dust in the house so he always showered at the Y before going home. He even spent an extra hour sometimes, especially lately, doing a few curls or sitting on a bike, or at least jawing with folks waiting at the machines. Tonight, though, he adds extra weight to the bar and lifts till it hurts.

When he's done, he drives west. Anthony and Ruth won't be expecting him. He should have called. He didn't know what to say, though, and thought if he just showed up they would get the picture. The light is fading and he turns down the wrong road in their half-built subdivision, then realizes his mistake. When he gets there, the house looks dark.

He rings the bell anyway and soon hears his brother's gravelly voice approaching the door. Anthony's got a drink in his hand and sips from the glass. Walt can smell the whiskey. Ruth is there, with a dim light from the kitchen behind her. She's got a drink, too.

"Patsy called," she says. "You might have told someone what you were up to. Before we called missing persons."

"Fix Walt a drink," Anthony says.

"You know he don't drink," she says, and fades back to the kitchen. Walt can't tell if she says that with disgust or admiration, but he doesn't much care. She kept Anthony from taking that promotion at DuPont because she didn't want to move away from her people, drags him to church meetings he doesn't want to go to, and generally bosses him around. "She's not our Momma," Walt used to tell him. "You don't have to listen to her." But Anthony kept his mouth shut.

"I need a place to stay," Walt says.

"We can't pick sides," Ruth calls from the kitchen.

Walt expects Anthony to say something about them being brothers, that it wasn't a question of taking sides, but he just shakes his head and points at the couch.

"You think it'll be long?"

"No," Walt says, only because he senses that's the right answer.

Ruth doesn't do anything about sheets, but Anthony finds them in a closet. Walt's used to sleeping on the couch, it's been that way at his house for a while now, so he slips a pillowcase over one of the cushions and settles in. Ruth says nothing to him on her way to their room in the back. He hears the door shut hard.

In the morning, Walt wakes up and sees his nephew, Jason, named for Ruth's daddy, in pale blue pajamas and clutching a grimy stuffed pig, his face only a foot or so away from Walt's. The boy's blinking at him, brown eyes wide, snot crusted on his lip, a pudgy hand inching toward Walt's nose.

"Hi there, buddy," Walt says softly, and Jason grins, snatches back his hand. Two tiny teeth poke up in the boy's gums. Walt never noticed before how much the boy looks like Anthony, with the dimpled chin, the smallish ears snug against his square head. Walt reaches for him and Jason runs away, giggling, to hide behind the liquor cabinet. He peeks out, giggles, peeks out again, then runs forward and leaps, landing on Walt's hip. He grabs the boy and tickles, buries his head in Jason's soft arms and breathes in his hypnotic, sour scent.

Ruth makes pancakes. "Jason likes them," she says, and Walt is surprised because he thought she was more of a cold cereal gal. Jason waves his fork in one hand and picks up syrupy squares of pancake with the other. His chin is a sticky mess, and his cheeks glow. Jason's eyes are on Walt, even while his fingers search his plate.

He's late to work and Don is waiting for him. Walt wonders if Don expects him to fail, to go back to the way he was before. He doesn't really know Don that well. Don sure doesn't know him. Walt wonders if everyone expects him to fail.

At lunch he finds a pay phone, at the McDonald's next to the Exxon station across the Interstate. He calls his own number, not exactly sure what he's going to say to Patsy but thinking he needs to at least tell her where he's staying. Probably Ruth already has done this, but she should hear it from him. There's no answer.

After cleaning up at the Y, he heads west. Past the crossroads and beyond the first set of hills he spots a wake of vultures, boiling around some carcass. Not the deer he had to leave in his pasture on Sunday, after it died a slow death, stranded on the barbed-wire fence while Walt waited for Patsy, that's south of here, and probably just bones by now. This corpse is new. Walt wonders what happens to a man who dies alone, an old farmer working his fields out of sight, no one at home to come looking. Do the birds find him? Do they rip away the overalls to get at the rotting flesh?

Ruth is feeding Jason when Walt comes in, and his presence distracts the boy. Ruth flings the spoon on the table and fixes herself a highball. Walt takes her place, dips the spoon in the macaroni, zooms it around Jason's head, and lands it in his mouth. Jason chews and laughs at the same time. Ruth watches and sips her drink.

"Does Patsy know I'm here?" he asks.

"She does," Ruth says.

Next day on the way to work there's no sign of the vultures, and none on the way back either. No sign of a corpse. No sign that anything happened.

On Friday night, Anthony's drinking a beer on the porch when Walt gets back. He and Don finished up at the retirement home on Tuesday, then landscaped a big new house at the north end of the county and filled in the week with mowing jobs. Walt's got his paycheck in his pocket. It's a pleasant evening, with a pink-edged sky and a breeze stirring the trees. He can hear Ruth and Jason inside, through the screen door. Ruth is reading to him, and he's babbling like he's reading, too. Anthony goes to get Walt a Coke.

He's smiling when he sits down again, and Walt's sure it's because of Jason. Walt smiles along with him.

"It makes all the difference in the world," Anthony says. He sips his beer, tilts back in his chair and looks up. There's a jet trail way high that looks like a long, straight highway.

"Nobody tells you how to make it, Brother. I sure didn't learn from our folks. Not Pop anyway." He chuckles and Walt joins in, but it's a wistful little laugh. "There ain't no roadmaps."

"I don't need a map, Tony. All's I want is a sign. Just a little sign." They laugh again.

The screen door creaks open and Ruth appears, with Jason clinging to her leg. "Supper's ready," she says.

The dishes washed and Jason put to bed, the three of them sit on the porch, listening to dueling crickets and bullfrogs. The more Walt concentrates, the louder they seem. He closes his eyes, and the noise is unbearable. But then there's a car approaching, tires spinning on gravel, and the night sounds vanish. Molly's Grand Am, Patsy behind the wheel, pulls into the drive.

She forgets to turn off the headlights when she climbs out and they cast twin beacons on the garage door, the reflected glow sending long shadows across the yard. She strides up the walk, pauses at the porch steps, steadies herself with a hand on the railing. She's wearing a light blue dress with skinny shoulder straps. There are black streaks under her eyes. Walt stands.

"You fucking bastard," she says, her voice loud.

"You'll wake Jason," Walt says, pointing to an open window.

"You fucking bastard coward." She's even louder now, and moves onto the first step. "Didn't have the balls to tell me to my face."

"You saw it coming. We couldn't go on that way."

"You spineless piece of shit." She takes another step up.

Anthony rises out of his chair. "Now, Patsy. Take it easy."

"Don't tell me to take it easy." She's on the porch now. "You're no better."

"This is none of our business, Anthony," Ruth says, and pulls him inside.

"What do you want from me?" Walt asks. His voice is low. The night has cooled, and Patsy is shivering. He moves toward her with his arms open. She steps back.

He takes another step. He doesn't smell booze on her breath.

"You never cried," she says, crying, and pounds her fist on his chest. He moves closer and she pounds his chest again. "I did it all alone."

"Patsy." He tries to take her in his arms but she pulls away, stumbles, runs down the steps. "You were never alone."

She turns back to face him. She's wiping tears from her cheek.

"Are you coming home?" she asks. He closes his eyes and he can hear the crickets again, and the bullfrogs. He thinks he can hear Jason's breathing, untroubled, strong.

"I was lost," he says, and stands on the porch, watching her climb into the car and slip into the night.

In the morning, Walt folds the sheets and takes the case off the cushion. He stuffs them into the hamper in the bathroom. Ruth's making oatmeal, even though it's a hot morning, and Jason is banging his spoon on his high chair. Anthony's at the table with the newspaper and coffee.

After breakfast, Walt helps with the dishes and drapes the towel on the oven door. He gives Jason a noisy kiss on the cheek and the boy laughs. Walt does it again. He heads out to his truck with his bundle of clothes and waves to Ruth and Anthony. Jason runs into the yard, stops and blows Walt a kiss.

Walt's not sure what to expect. He doesn't know how he can explain it to Patsy, or how he can help make her understand what he wants. He doesn't know where they're going. There's no way of knowing. But there's too much ahead of them that they shouldn't miss out on. And somebody's got to take the first step.

THE NYMPH AND THE WOODSMAN

*Then the deer came out from under the pile of
wood where it had been hiding, not daring to
breathe, and thanked the woodcutter for his
kindness . . .* —Asian Folktale

1.

On the day after his momma's funeral, Bobby Cabe pulls a creased snapshot from his wallet and plunks it on the bar: Bobby Jr. way back when he was five, barefoot and muddy, big grin on his freckled face, holding baby Tulip's hand. Bobby turns the picture so Dwight can see.

"Ain't they something?"

"You need to go get 'em," says Dwight, elbows on the bar. The red neon Bud sign in the window reflects off Dwight's bald head. "Bring 'em back where they belong."

"Not that simple," says Bobby. He fires up another smoke and lets the match burn in the crowded ashtray. It's been a dozen years. He didn't lift a finger when Belle left, he stayed behind with Momma, and now it's too late. He watches Dwight pull a bottle of Jack from under the bar, pour himself a shot, and throw it back. Damn, Bobby thinks, how can I get me a job like that, paid to stand around, all the gas you can guzzle.

"Time like this, a man needs his family."

Been gone so long, I don't know where to start. Bobby's not sure whether he's said the words out loud, but he looks up at Dwight, waits for a response.

2.

Back in '68, home from Vietnam a year, Bobby camped in the trailer behind his momma's tin-roofed cabin, deep up Barren Hollow. A man's got to work, his momma pestered, so he put in at the tailpipe factory where his daddy had welded until a skid of pipes mashed his skull. But they'd just laid off another shift and there was no place for Bobby.

He got by, though. Sometimes old Dallas Doak wanted a digger on a fence job, and that was steady for a few days. Or John Craig's daddy needed a hand at the forge, seeing as how John was in college down at Blacksburg and didn't come home much anymore. He heard John had found himself a girl from Roanoke. That boy had it made, hadn't got blood on his hands and up his nose in some fucking gook village.

Mostly—the only work close to regular—Bobby cut wood. Seemed no end to the bad trees folks didn't want to tackle, or bother their own boys with. So Bobby'd get the word—a pin oak on the ridge was down, or the blight's found another stand of chestnuts. He'd haul saws and ropes up the mountain and he'd be a one-man band, biting through bark, filling his lungs with sawdust, rubbing his hands raw. It felt good, like he was getting somewhere.

But woodcutting was lonely work. Most days Bobby didn't see a soul, least not the flesh and blood variety. More than once, his daddy stopped by, looking none the worse for the gully across his head. Matthew Payne paid a visit, another local boy who'd landed in the paddies, sent home in pieces after that grenade fell in his lap. Bobby had laid down his saw and was taking a smoke break when Matthew sat right next to him on a log. One after another those boys came. Jesse Armstrong, grinning like he always did, as if that sniper bullet hadn't tunneled through his brain. Squirrel Jackson, even in high school busy with the ladies and the football team called him Squirrel 'cause he was always burying his nuts. Knifed over a Saigon whore.

3.

"You need to go get 'em," Dwight says again. He draws Bobby another beer.

Bobby shakes his head, has a clouded vision of being pulled over as he loops down the pike, but drinks anyway, listening to the football on TV, half thinking of his momma curled up in her coffin, half watching a pink-haired girl at the bar. She inhales a shot of schnapps, winces and rattles her head like she swallowed medicine. She's his daughter's age now, maybe a couple years older, but still too young. Bobby wants to tell her to go home to her daddy.

4.

It got so Bobby looked forward to seeing those ghosts. He'd be up before dawn, hear his momma spit and cough over in the shack or turn on that radio she kept by the sink, and slip into the woods before she had a chance to nag him about whatever was on her mind—no coffee in the larder or her trash needed carting to the landfill. Not that he minded doing for her. She'd had it rough with Bobby's hard-luck daddy, and now she spent dawn to dark working on her place, sweeping the boundless dirt, patching and mending, coaxing a garden from the stony soil.

On his way up the mountain one cold morning, head pounding from closing Rocky's the night before, there was barely enough light to see. But Bobby knew those woods like the rusty ceiling above his cot. He knew where the game trails wandered and where the stream trickled through the limestone from the spring in the high pasture. Downed leaves covered the path, soaked after a rainy fall but frosted on top, soft and brittle underfoot at the same time. Christmas was still a ways off, but the weather had turned. Solitary snow flakes nested in his beard. Ice rimmed the creek, and there were jaws of the stuff, icicle teeth and all, where the rocks churned the creek into foamy spray.

This jungle was nothing like 'Nam. Not steamy and rank with rotting boys and flies. Not cave-dark and out to kill, every step a blood-bath waiting to happen. A sniper, or a frag mine in the weeds, or under a smooth rock that looks safe and then you're gone, nothing. If not you, the next guy. If not him, them. In that village outside Tay Nanh, not just girls and old men, VC, too, a first for Bobby close range, he saw the gun and the kid's eyes, fired fast, saw the face explode.

But these woods were his. Sharp air and tangy pines, slow snow and the icy creek.

Bobby climbed, and heard voices. He worried about the tools he'd left up there, borrowed from Dallas Doak and nobody'd believe Bobby if he claimed they'd been stolen, least of all Dallas, who'd accused Bobby's daddy of poaching on his land, and tried to have his momma arrested for pilfering sweet corn right off the stalks. If those tools were missing, Bobby might as well keep walking, over that timber ridge and on to the next.

That's what Bobby was thinking when the bullet zinged by. He knew from the war his best place was down in the dirt. He huddled by a log, back in that jungle oven, braced for fire from the VC sniper, wondering who'd been hit. But no, his home woods, hunters, deer season in full swing. A trickle burned at his temple, fingertips scarlet. He made it to his knees, to his feet, crouched, kept on, away from the whispers.

5.

"Wouldn't know where to start," Bobby says to Dwight. Belle could have taken them anywhere.

"Maybe I oughtn't to say," Dwight says, swirling his rag on the bar, "but I believe I know where they're at."

Bobby sets his beer down and looks at Dwight. He crushes his cigarette in the ashtray and his hands tremble when he lights a new one.

"You been holding out on me, Dwight?" The smoke twists through Bobby's fingers like rope. "How long you known?"

"Not long," Dwight says. "Ran into her daddy. Hardly recognized him."

"I guess you better tell me," Bobby says.

Dwight, grinning, writes down an address on a napkin and slides it across the bar.

Bobby stares at the scrawl, just the name of a mountain town and a road, then stumbles off his barstool. He tips his cap to Dwight and pushes outside into the flurries, big flakes meandering, like feathers. He knows what he has to do. It's high time. Past time. The truck is meat-locker cold and the engine won't turn over. He rubs his hands together, chafed and numb, tries the engine again. With a gag and sputter the truck shakes, its low growl wobbly. He pulls out the snapshot and sets it on the dash. A feather lands on the windshield, and Bobby watches it disappear.

6.

Still bleeding, he crept deeper into the woods, away from the whispers, away from the guns. The brush shivered. A white tail flew past. He heard the crack of a rifle, and a shot pinged into a stout cedar. The voices behind him grew louder. Bobby ran after the deer, glancing back toward their pursuers. Crimson blazes darkened the tangled creeper. And then Bobby came upon him, shrinking into the bushes as if he could hide in the long-gone leaves, shoulder oozing blood. Steam puffed from his snout.

"Help me," said the deer.

The voices were close.

"Please," said the deer. The word was prolonged, desperate.

Moving fast, Bobby propped a fallen branch against the bushes, hiding the deer's flank. He snapped off a pine bough and mounted it through the antlers, twisting the needles until the trophy was invisible. He backed out of the brush, scuffed away hoof prints, stripped off twigs that bore the animal's blood, and turned to face the hunters.

"You're Bobby Cabe, ain't you?" asked one of the men, a fleshy farmer about Bobby's age. "Been awhile, Bobby. Heard you was back."

It was Clay Shifflet, somebody Bobby'd known a long time ago, enough to get into a scuffle with now and then after football games, grown stout and bearded. And an older man, Clay's daddy.

"See my twelve-pointer come through here, Bobby? Damn. I know I winged him. Has to be hurt."

"Fine looking animal, Clay. But I believe you're mistaken. He was moving good, like he seen a ghost." Bobby pointed east, where the sky was already bright. Clay nodded; the men ran off.

Bobby stepped back slowly, afraid they'd realize he'd lied. But the voices faded. Bobby uncovered the buck, pulled the branch from his rack, touched the crusting blood on the deer's shoulder, and saw that it wasn't a deer at all, but a gnarled little man in a cone hat, shoulders hunched, a wisp of gray beard drooping from his chin. Bobby blinked and rubbed his eyes. In that oozing Asian village there'd been a toothless man, shriveled and bent, begging for his life. Bobby had hesitated then, too, his weapon slipping in his sweaty hands, and watched while his prisoner disappeared into what had seemed a solid wall of jungle.

"Thank you, Bobby Cabe," said this man, brushing sodden leaves from his cloak. He gazed up through narrow slits and tapped Bobby's belly with a crooked finger. "I must repay your kindness by granting a wish. What is the one thing you want more than anything else?"

Bobby stared at the old man. And then it came to him.

"A beautiful woman—so beautiful all these boys, that Clay Shifflet, even John Craig down at the college with his Roanoke girl, will look at me like I won the lotto. A beautiful wife. And babies. That's what I want."

"Done." And the man told Bobby about the nymphs who bathed each morning in the pool at Barren Falls. "Steal the robe of one of the nymphs. She'll be stranded—unable to fly back to heaven with her sisters. She will be the most beautiful creature you have ever seen. She will arouse the envy of every man. But you must be careful—if they see you, they will leave and never return."

7.

Outside Rocky's, through the scrim of snow and beer, Bobby sees a white van parked in front of his pickup and a custom Viper inches behind. He bangs the truck into gear, goes easy on the gas but lurches into the van anyway. Twisting the wheel, he reverses, rocks back, and hears the crunch of glass when his tow hitch pokes out the Viper's headlight. He spins the tires forward, prepared to sideswipe the van if it comes to that, but he's finally clear. He races through the yellow light at Central and Main, and heads up the mountain to find his family.

8.

The talking deer had vanished, and then the old man, and Bobby wondered if he'd seen them at all. But blood stained his fingers and boots, and the little man's raspy voice was clear in his head. So Bobby trekked up the mountain. He followed the creek to the falls, shivered behind a boulder at the edge of the pool, and waited. Soon he heard them, a trio of voices soft and sweet as bees, buzzing at the water's edge. Despite the early December chill, three beauties—one with long chestnut hair tied back, one with thick blond plaits piled high, one with raven curls—waded waist deep in the icy pool, splashed like schoolgirls, scrubbed each other's backs with strips of bark, let the waterfall stream over their sleek shoulders and cascade from their breasts. While the women frolicked in the pool, Bobby sneaked around the bank, peeking from behind rocks and trees, always remembering the old man's warning. But they were so magnificent, these women of his dreams, that he couldn't help himself and raised his head to get a better look.

His foot slipped. A rock tumbled into the water.

"Who's there?" asked one of the voices.

Bobby sank behind the rocks, holding his breath as he'd done on patrol in the jungle. But the laughter and splashing returned, a steady hum on the breeze.

At the edge of the forest, where the pond flowed into the stream to begin its run down the mountain, Bobby found the robes, spread, like dew, over the bramble. He reached out a trembling hand. The closest robe, stitched from feathers as soft as clouds, was a blizzard of the purest white, the next one a pale blue, the color of the haze on the mountains. The voices from the pool were singing now, no words, just a ghostly melody.

"Steal a robe," the old man had said.

9.

The flurries become a pelting gale and the road ices. At the crossroads west of town, Bobby goes straight toward the mountains instead of turning south to Barren Hollow Road and the gravel track up to his place. Nothing for him there—his momma gone, work dried up, the trailer peeled open like a tin can from the rust and hellish wind. No point in holding on to ghosts and memories; Bobby wants his flesh and blood.

10.

Bobby set his hand on the third robe, bright yellow, rich as a field of mustard flowers. He'd never felt anything softer, not the long grass he'd rolled in as a boy, or the creek moss where he'd lain and stared up at the clouds. He tucked the blanket of feathers under his arm and ran. Breathing hard, Bobby buried the robe under a mound of pine boughs and returned to the pool. The buzz turned like a saw now, the sweet hum gone bitter. Two robed nymphs hovered just above the ground, worried eyes hunting for the missing yellow robe, while one lone beauty sobbed on her knees in the shallows. A shaft of golden light struck the pond, and the nymphs rose: first the white robe, then the blue. The light dissolved, leaving the forlorn girl.

"You all right, Miss?" Bobby stepped out of hiding, half-ashamed, but struck by the woman's perfection. She tried to cover herself, but he could see her firm, round breasts, the silky, wet skin, almost as soft and yellow as the robe he'd stolen. Her almond eyes, deep purple with flecks of gold, rained tears.

"Have you seen my yellow robe?" asked the nymph.

Bobby averted his gaze. "No, Miss. Haven't seen a robe." He took a step forward, pulled off his drab jacket and held it out to her. "You better put this on."

They sat together on the rocks, Bobby recognizing mistrust in the nymph's eyes. She feared him, like the Saigon ladies with their shopping baskets and high-collared *ao dai* who crossed the street to avoid a G.I. like him.

She raised her eyes and lowered them again. "My name is Đẹp Nhất," she said, almost in a whisper. "It means 'Beauty.'"

"I'll look after you, Beauty," Bobby said, and took hold of her velvety hand.

11.

The hunter's bullet that nicked Bobby's head awoke all the dark war memories and crazy dreams: one with snakes crawling out of his insides like guts, and another where the gun in his hand went off but it was himself he'd shot, and he watched his own body crumple like some flag that had lost its wind. That one kept coming back. He died over and over again.

Rocky's was the only place where he could forget. One winter night he sat at the bar, drowning the ghosts and the dreams. The door swung open, a cold gust swirled around his legs, and a greasy kid in leather scuffed inside, trailing a platinum-haired girl. The pair climbed the barstools like they'd been in the tavern a hundred times. The girl hesitated, as if she thought the boy might help her off with her ripped camouflage jacket, but he was busy lighting a cigarette and she peeled it off herself. Bobby scooted over so he could see her legs, stubby things that stuck out of her red miniskirt like tree roots in a sidewalk; his eyes popped up to a chest that swelled a bright pink sweater. Bobby shook his head and smoked, and just then the girl looked his way.

She came in the next night, without the greaser, and Bobby was glad he'd shaved and had washed his shirt. He felt the heat rise in his gut when she winked at him. She sat in the same spot, smoked a cigarette, pushed her chest out, and when Bobby made no move she picked up her beer and sidled over.

"I'm Belle," she said.

They had a few drinks, until Bobby's cash was gone, and then went out to his truck. She let him open her blouse, slip a hand up her skirt. Bobby put his mouth on her neck, didn't mind the brown roots under that white hair, smelled perfume that made him think of booze more than flowers, but that just excited him more. He pushed her down on the seat. She unzipped his pants.

Months later, Bobby was still sitting at Rocky's fighting off those dreams where he died over and over. Belle came in again, in a yellow cotton frock that couldn't hide her swollen belly, followed by a leathery man in stained overalls and a matted, gray beard. They stepped up to Bobby. The man took off his hat. Belle grinned.

"Bobby Cabe, meet my daddy."

12.

After the wedding they settled into the trailer and lived on a steady diet of too much drink and no money to speak of. Bobby's momma put Belle to work cleaning and cooking. Soon, Bobby Jr. came along, and the next year his little sister, called Tulip.

At least old Rocky and the new bartender, Dwight, were good listeners. They'd let Bobby moan about how hard life was, between Belle's jealous sniping and his momma's orneriness, the screaming babies, and the ghosts of his daddy and Matthew and the others. Bobby even tried to tell Dwight about the talking deer who changed into a gnome with a pointy hat, and about Beauty, how there'd been a goddess in his life once, before Belle.

"You're one hell of a yarn spinner, Bobby Cabe," Dwight said, and hooted. "Like one of those old-timey folk. That's rich—a talking deer."

13.

"I'm going back to my Daddy," Belle threatened, after Bobby'd stumbled home from Rocky's one night smelling of sweet perfume. "You're worthless trash, Bobby Cabe. I swear I'm going and I'll take those babies with me."

"You'll be sorry if you do," Bobby yelled.

14.

Bobby knows he's doing the right thing after all these years. He's going to find Tulip and Bobby Jr. and bring them home where they belong. He pulls the truck off the road. The snow is heavier now, but not sticking, except where it catches in cold furrows and the tall, dead grass. He hops a ditch into the cornfield, lands on a cob that snaps under his boot, unzips and pisses while he stares straight up and lets the flakes settle on his face. Then it's back in the truck and on up the mountain.

15.

Belle turned a blind eye, and, for a while, the trailer was peaceful. Bobby never tired of Tulip's mud pie tea parties or Bobby Jr.'s chatter, how he'd carry on whole conversations with forest critters, imaginary or otherwise. Bobby passed on what his father had taught him about the woods: the seventeen varieties of pine trees native to their county, how to husk a walnut without permanently staining your fingers black, why the moss grew only on one side of the trees. He worked hard at odd jobs around the holler, but if there was no work, Bobby'd be just as happy with those two, exploring the mountain, Tulip up on his shoulders, Bobby Jr. right by his side. Bobby tried to interest Belle in those things, too, but it would take Bobby Jr. tugging Belle's hands, or Tulip sobbing at Belle's knees, for her to come with them to see the gray football of a hornets' nest dangling from a sycamore, or the swarm of yellow swallowtails that set the pasture in motion, or the red creeper in autumn, wrapped around a locust tree like a shiny Christmas ribbon.

One evening Bobby sat with Bobby Jr. and Tulip on the steps of the trailer. They watched the darkness fall and the lightning bugs blossom like wildflowers. Inside, Belle hummed while she dried the supper dishes. Bobby hummed along.

"Did I ever tell you kids about the Nymph and the Woodsman?"

Bobby Jr. and Tulip shook their heads, and Bobby proceeded to tell the story of how the lonely woodsman saved a talking deer from hunters, and how the deer changed into a little man.

"Like an elf?" asked Tulip.

"More like a gnome," said Bobby. "Anyway, that old man told the woodsman where he could find a beautiful nymph to be his wife." Bobby heard Belle's footsteps, saw the broad shadow she cast, and knew she was listening at the trailer door.

"What was her name?" asked Tulip, her eyes struggling to stay open.

"Her name was 'Beauty,'" Bobby said.

When Bobby Jr. and Tulip were asleep, and Belle was settled in front of the television, Bobby slipped out and headed down to Rocky's. And when Bobby came back from Rocky's and tried to cozy up to her ("Get away from me, you think I don't know where you've been?"), the first thing Belle threw at him ("Whose cheap perfume is that?") was the plastic ashtray he'd won for her at the county fair ("This house is filled with trash, just like you!"), and when that just bounced off the side of his head without so much as leaving a mark ("You're a worthless lying skunk!"), she picked up a skillet ("I'm sick and tired of hearing about that 'Beauty' woman you've been messing with!") and beaned Bobby good, right on that old scar above his eye.

When he came around, Belle was gone, and Bobby Jr. and Tulip, too.

16.

The snow is falling in earnest at Bison Gap, groaning under Bobby's tires, a solid wall caught in his headlights. He drives blind at the top of the mountain, needs to piss again, hands icy, eyelids drooping. He feels himself swerve, and swings back to his side of the road, except he can't see lines anymore, just white-blue, and not even tire tracks to follow. Got to stop before I drive over the edge, Bobby thinks. Drop a mile into the valley and disappear. What the hell, who'd even notice if Bobby Cabe ain't ever heard from again? Might be exciting for a second, flying in the dark like the Ford has wings, and maybe we keep on flying. Better than freezing to death in a rust bucket at the side of a lonely road. Worth a shot.

But he lets the truck slow and steers to the edge. The snow falls hard, piling on the wipers, building mounds that soon cover the windshield. Bobby pulls his jacket tighter, jams his hands in his pockets, and lays his head against the window.

17.

"I wish I could go home," Beauty said sometimes, eyes drifting skyward. Bobby tried to forget that home for her was a misty cloud. Whenever she said it, the babies looked up at her with their worried, angelic faces.

Once, Beauty had such a forlorn look that Bobby almost told her where he'd buried her robe. But he saw how the years hadn't aged her a day, the eyes still that unnatural iris color, with the drop of yellow when the light hit right, her lush brown hair still glowing like the moon.

It had been years since Bobby had been to the pool by the waterfall where he'd first seen Beauty, but old man Doak had passed away and Miz Doak needed trees cleared. Bobby trooped up the mountain, stopping now and then to breathe in the hypnotic smell of cedar or pluck a sprig of calming mountain mint to chew. He thought he heard steps behind him, but when he turned to look for hunters or that magic deer, he saw nothing. Finally, he came to the pool and looked at his own reflection in the water: grizzled and stewed, a cigarette in his mouth and a moldy cap pulled over his eyes. An old man, almost, married to the saddest, most beautiful girl in the county. He backed away and came to the pile of branches he'd made so long before. One by one he pulled them off, until the yellow robe appeared, glowing like new fire.

"I should have known." Beauty stood behind him, hands on hips, her face blazing red, the babies clutching her skirt.

"I can explain," Bobby said.

"You lied to me, Bobby Cabe." She snatched the robe out of his hands, and when she wrapped it around her shoulders a shaft of golden light fell at her feet. Bobby lunged at her, grasping for the babies. She lifted Bobby Jr. and Tulip into her arms and, without looking back, rose to heaven.

18.

The truck window thunders in Bobby's ear. He opens his eyes to see a gloved hand brushing snow from his windshield and an icy face peering in. The hand pounds again.

"You okay, Mister?" The voice is muted.

Bobby shivers and realizes how cold he is, moves his hands and winces when he bends his trembling fingers around the lock. The door opens.

"You like to've froze, Mister." It's a young voice, not quite a man, a knit cap pulled low, almost covering his eyes, flecks of ice in the black weave. The boy nudges Bobby across the seat, closes the door and turns the key. "Heat work in this thing?"

The engine coughs, but comes to life. The boy pulls off the hat, lets his lush brown hair tumble out. Bobby can't stop shaking. The air blowing from the heater is cold, but, slowly, the cab fills with warmth. The boy looks at Bobby. His eyes are iris, with a glint of yellow.

"You live around here, boy?" The feeling has come back to Bobby's hands, and he can wiggle his toes inside his boots.

"Just up the mountain. Got a cabin, me and my momma and sister."

"Got a daddy?"

"Course I got a daddy," the boy says and snickers. "Everybody's got a daddy."

"Must be a handsome feller to make a boy like you." Bobby can't take his eyes away from those eyes.

The boy's face darkens and he squirms behind the wheel. "Look, Mister, if you're okay, I best be going." When Bobby nods, the boy pushes the door open against the wind. Bobby watches him knife into the blowing snow.

19.

The night Bobby's wife ran off with the babies, Bobby's momma pounded on the trailer door.

"Where'd that little witch get to? A body'd starve."

Bobby didn't look at her, didn't look up from the pile of toys he'd whittled, the toy soldiers and crude pistol for the boy, the whistle and a puppet for the girl.

"She's gone, Momma."

"Something unnatural about that girl. Good riddance, I say."

20.

Bobby pulls a pint bottle from under the seat of the truck. It warms him some. The wind shifts and he sees the boy again, watches him trudge through the snow, down the road and then straight uphill, nimble, climbing fast.

21.

When Bobby saw the stag a second time, he couldn't believe it was the same animal, all those years later. But what the hell, he thought, who's to say a magic deer ain't immortal? The stag recognized him, too, even though Bobby had grown a round gut and a long beard, and had lost a tooth or two to brawls and bad habits.

"Is that you, Bobby Cabe?" The animal pawed the dirt between them and lowered his crown. When he raised his head, it was the old man's eyes that stared back at Bobby.

"I see," said the little man. "She found the robe."

"Please help me," Bobby said. "I've got to get them back. I've lost everything."

"I remember your kindness, Bobby Cabe." The man looked around as if to make sure no one else was listening. "You must fly to her and beg her forgiveness. If she looks into your heart and sees the depth of your remorse, she may return. Go back to the pool beneath the waterfall. Then whistle. And wait."

Bobby strode up the mountain. He stood at the water's edge, boots sinking into the muck, whistled and heard his melody echo back. The tune swelled. Wind rippled across the pool, the forest swayed, and as a shaft of light fell at his feet, Bobby heard a deafening roar. A tiger descended the beam, snarled and bowed his head, but kept one eye on Bobby. Bobby didn't move. His daddy had told tales of big panthers in those hills, some with magical powers, but there was no mistaking this striped jungle cat from the stories he'd heard in 'Nam. The animal went down on his knees; Bobby held one hand over its brawny neck and felt the steam rise. The tiger lifted his head as if inviting Bobby to mount, and Bobby did. The tiger leapt.

22.

Bobby wakes to a cleared road, a plowed heap locking the truck against the hillside. He jumps out and sets to work with his hands digging snow away from the tires and front bumper. When he's done he climbs inside, drinks again from the bottle, and looks up the mountain.

He finds the road he wants, rutted and unplowed, twisting above Bison Gap between timber stands and a sheer drop. At a switchback he loses traction. He pumps the brakes, goes into a skid, thinks again he's headed over the edge and—stops, the butt of the truck against a pine that shakes, dropping its mantle of snow in a fresh blizzard.

Bobby takes another swig, stumbles out of the truck and jams his hands in his pockets. The boy's deep prints cross the road and disappear into the trees. Bobby tries to follow, hanging onto branches, grabbing at rocks to haul himself up, scraping his numb fingers on sharp edges, leaden and clumsy where the boy seemed to fly. The hill is so steep, and the snow-covered footing so uncertain, that he moves handhold to handhold, sometimes on his knees. He's done this before. This is something he knows.

23.

The tiger landed on a cloud, in front of a vine-covered cottage. A dense garden of daylilies and yellow roses stretched along a picket fence as far as Bobby could see; a flock of goldfinches twittered in a brassy maple. The cottage door stood open. Beauty rocked and sewed by a stone hearth. The girl at her feet sketched flowers on butter-colored paper. The boy turned the pages of his picture book in the golden light of the bay window.

Beauty didn't look up when Bobby stepped inside, and the children paid no notice. Hot chocolate simmered on the stove, its scent braided with the smell of fresh-baked bread.

"You're my wife," Bobby said. "You'll come back with me."

Beauty's expression didn't change as she moved her sewing closer to her eyes, folded the cloth across her lap, and pulled a stitch tight. The girl had snuggled with a stuffed rabbit and closed her eyes, breathing evenly, a smile on her face. The boy stared out the window at swallowtails cavorting in the garden.

"You hear me?" Bobby shouted. "I have nothing. You've got to come home."

Beauty stopped rocking. She settled her sewing basket by the fire and rose, lifted her skirt to step over the girl, ladled a cup of cocoa at the stove, took it to the boy.

"Do you hear me?"

Beauty caressed the boy's long brown curls while he sniffed at the rising vapors.

24.

Bobby finds the boy's tracks and resumes the steep climb. Then the land settles back, the road lost in milky drifts. He follows the trail through the woods to a clearing, just a breath between soaring pines, with a steep drop to the valley floor beyond. Snow blankets a cabin at the clearing's edge; smoke curls from the stone chimney. The boy raises an ax and the echo of his chop shoots across the clearing as the split log falls. He raises the ax over and over. A girl pops out of the cabin and watches the boy work, then scoops up a ball of snow and throws it at him. Bobby hears the buzz of her laughter from where he hides in the trees and her shriek when the boy returns fire. Then the girl holds out her arms and the boy piles on wood until she sags. She goes inside and comes back for more.

A short woman with white-blond hair follows her out of the cabin.

25.

"Do you hear me, Beauty?" Bobby shouted again.

Beauty looked up at him.

26.

Waving to Bobby Jr. and Tulip, Belle wraps a red scarf around her throat, slips a basket over her arm and heads into the woods. Bobby takes a long gulp from his pint bottle, and strides across the clearing.

"Hey, Mister," says the boy, leaning on the ax. "Guess you're okay."

"Hello," says the girl, half hiding her smile behind a mittened hand.

"I want to thank you for your help before," says Bobby.

The boy nods. Bobby looks into the woods and sees no sign of Belle.

"I wonder if you could help me again, you and your pretty sister here. It's my truck." He'll lure them down to the pickup, they'll climb inside to get warm, and somehow, he hasn't figured that part out yet, he'll keep them inside and take off and they'll live with him and they'll forget about Belle. Or Belle will come to find them and stay, too, because she'll realize how much he needs them all and things will be different now. A man ought to be with his family. The boy raises the ax over his head and lodges it in the chopping block. He tucks his hair under his cap. Bobby and Bobby Jr. look to Tulip, doubt twinkling in her lavender eyes, her cheeks coloring; but she links her arm in her brother's and the three of them set off.

27.

"I've been expecting you, Bobby Cabe," said Beauty. The girl was awake now and hugged her mother's knees. "I knew you'd come."

"You're going back with me. All of you. You belong with me."

"You lied, Bobby Cabe. You stole my robe. I will not go back."

28.

Tulip lays her head on her brother's broad shoulder, kicks her boots through the deep snow in the clearing. The boy smiles at Bobby.

Belle runs from the woods, spilling her basket of nuts and berries.

29.

Bobby lunged at Beauty. He snatched up the boy in one arm, the girl in the other, and tore out of the cottage, through the golden flower beds and over the picket fence, to the tiger crouched at the edge of the cloud.

30.

Belle levels a .12 gauge Winchester at Bobby. She edges forward. "Get away from my babies, Bobby Cabe. I'll shoot, I swear I will."

"They're not babies no more, Belle." Bobby grips Bobby Jr.'s elbow and pulls Tulip to his side. "They can come with me if they want to." Bobby Jr. tries to free his arm but Bobby digs in his fingers and won't let go. "They need to know their daddy."

"Let go of Tulip, Mister," Bobby Jr. pleads. He grabs at Bobby with his free hand.

Tulip slams the toe of her boot into Bobby's knee and it buckles, just enough to let her wriggle out of his grasp. She pumps her arms and plows through the snow to the cabin.

"I want my girl, Belle. Y'all come down the mountain with me." He inches back, pulling Bobby Jr. with him, the two of them digging blue troughs in the drift.

Belle closes the gap.

"Put that thing away, Belle. You don't want to hurt our boy do you?" He yanks Bobby Jr. closer, and just as he does the boy shoves the heel of his free hand into Bobby's chin. Bobby drops his arms to break his backward fall. Bobby Jr. springs away.

Belle raises the shotgun and aims at Bobby's head.

31.

Bobby jumped on the tiger's back, almost losing his hold on the girl, and struggled to hang on to the squirming boy. The tiger roared and rose on its hind legs, mauling the air.

32.

"Now, Belle, don't you go getting any crazy notions. You can't shoot an unarmed man, can you? I just wanted to see them children you stole away from me."

"Bobby Cabe, you whoring dog. You got no right. Now, get up this minute and crawl back into your hole."

Bobby scrambles to his feet, skids in the snow, recovers his balance. He thinks a wife oughtn't to threaten her husband like that. He jumps toward her.

33.

The tiger bucked, and both babies slipped from Bobby's grasp, into the cloud. As Bobby clung to the cat's dense fur it sprang toward the shaft of light.

34.

Belle pulls the trigger. The blast echoes in the clearing, and booms in Bobby's ears.

"You go on now, Bobby Cabe," Belle says as she stands over him and pumps the shotgun. He lies in the snow, fingertips hovering over the wound, a trickle of blood, no more than a column of ants, marching down his cheek. "Next time I won't miss."

35.

As the tiger descended the light, Bobby saw the cloud above him evaporate. The mountain came up to meet him, the pool at Barren Falls a gaping mouth, the splashing white waterfall calling to him. Just above the pond the tiger bucked again and sent Bobby plunging into the icy depths.

36.

Bobby lurches to his feet. "Junior," he calls. "Tulip?"

Bobby Jr. keeps his eyes on the snow. Tulip peeks from behind the cabin door. Belle lowers the shotgun, still trained on Bobby, and steps forward. Bobby takes a step back. He sees the dream again, the one where he dies over and over, doesn't really mind that the time has finally come. It's high time. Past time. Belle takes another step. And on they go to the edge of the clearing, a sheer drop at Bobby's heels. Belle's eyes glint yellow in the sun.

"Beauty?" Bobby asks, shielding his eyes. "I'm truly sorry about your yellow robe."

Bobby sees his babies romping in wildflowers, the cottage curtains rustling through open windows. He smells bread and chocolate. Beauty stands in the door, the feathered robe draped on her shoulders. "Beauty?" Bobby asks again, his family in reach. Her mouth moves but he can't hear the words. He's welcome to stay, he believes she's saying. She raises the gun. Bobby Jr. is waving and calling to him, running to meet him, shouting words Bobby can't hear.

Bobby leaps toward Beauty, his arms outstretched.

HEADING FOR HOME

It seemed to Deputy Albert Halliwell that summer's long days and balmy breezes brought out the worst in folks. He'd lived in the Valley his whole life, and that's the way it had always been. Even so, Albert prayed this summer he could make time to spend with DeShawn. The boy needed him.

On the last Saturday in June, when Albert planned to slip away early to DeShawn's baseball game, the 911 dispatcher took a call from Jeremiah Cochran, something about a killing on his high pasture. After the old man screamed "Murder!" into the phone, the frenzy in the sheriff's office barely wilted when it turned out the deceased was a cow, a member of Cochran's Black Angus herd. Albert suppressed a smile as the truth finally dawned, and chided himself for thinking the killing of a cow in the heart of a farming community was anything but serious. The Sheriff sent Albert and the new man, Sonny Chambers, out to investigate.

Albert's like of pretty much every man, woman, and child he knew did not yet extend to Sonny. The rookie was from a small town just up the pike, in the shadow of the Blue Ridge, which qualified him as a local boy. But he'd gone north to college and, when that didn't take, spent time in the Army, then knocked around Texas for a while when it turned out a military career was not for him either. Albert couldn't put his finger on it, but he didn't trust the man, didn't like the way he smoked his cigarettes cupped in the palm of his hand, or the grease that poufed up his hair in front.

And then there was the way he rolled his eyes whenever Albert told him to do anything. Albert didn't feel good about letting those little things bother him, but the way he saw it, they added up.

DeShawn would be disappointed—another game missed. The boy had been staying with Albert and Sheryl and the baby close to a year, half of last summer and right through ninth grade. He was Albert's cousin, or anyway his Aunt Denise's boy, or maybe a grandbaby by Denise's wild girl, Debby, who called herself by some other name now, as if that would wipe away the dope and the stealing. Or maybe he was Sandra's, the good one, whose only crime was getting pregnant—twice—before her sixteenth birthday. Aunt Denise had decided Northeast D.C. was no place for DeShawn, that the gangs or the drugs were going to kill him, one way or another. Besides, it would do him no good to go on living in a cramped apartment full of women and babies, with no men to look up to except the ones on the street corner or the ones Debby and Sandra settled for. And there was Albert in that big house in the small town, a fine job and a uniform. Everybody agreed, all those women, that it was the perfect place for DeShawn.

Not that Albert minded. The boy was family, and life was good. The badge had mostly put an end to the trash talk he'd heard growing up, and folks didn't seem to pay much attention anymore to the fact that he was black. He knew they still whispered, gritted their teeth at the sight of him, maybe complained how he'd been promoted because of his skin. Some boy whose uncle was county supervisor should have had the job, they probably said. But at least they wouldn't say it to his face. Most days, if he had to, he could close his eyes and pretend it wasn't a problem.

On the drive out to the Cochran place, Albert told Sonny what it was all about.

"A cow?" Sonny lit a cigarette and rolled down the window. "We're investigating a murdered cow?"

"Yeah, it's a pisser. But don't let Old Man Cochran hear you laughing. It's a big deal to him. Understand?" Albert turned away so Sonny wouldn't see his own grin.

"But—a cow?" Sonny's laughter filled the car with smoke. Cochran was waiting in front of his barn, a ramshackle contraption that used to be red, Albert remembered, with a faded Virginia Tech logo painted on the broad side where it might have been visible from the road if a barrier of pine trees hadn't grown up in front. It looked to Albert as if the barn had been around almost as long as the old man, maybe longer—they both leaned to one side like they were on their way downhill. Over black-rimmed glasses, Cochran peered at Albert head to toe, then looked at Sonny, back at Albert and, although he seemed to recognize Albert, he addressed himself to Sonny. One white man to another. Albert knew the old guy didn't mean any harm by it. It's just the way he was.

Albert had grown up on the town's West End, where most of the black families lived, and where the black high school used to be—a community center now that the county had solved the integration problem by building consolidated schools that nobody could argue with. He'd been in the transition year back then, one day part of a black student sea, isolated but comfortable, and the next made to feel like an oil slick in somebody else's ocean, to be contained, scrubbed clean. There'd been a few incidents, almost all because a white parent was unhappy about something or other— blacks and whites in the same choir, or gym class, or school play. But the kids seemed to manage pretty well, most of them, taking it slow, mixing at the edges until they were all part of one another. That seemed like a good thing, to Albert.

Not all the black kids felt the same way. There was one boy, taller than the others and older, whose family had come up from Mississippi. Ruben was always angry about something, about the school dress code, about the coaches, all white, who grudgingly put the black boys on the team but would only play whites in games, about the black janitor who everybody pretended was invisible. "We got to fight back," he'd said. "We got to take what's ours." For Albert, though, it didn't make sense to get so worked up. It was going to take time, anybody could see that, and it was better than before. "Let's be patient, Ruben," he'd counseled.

Looking back, Albert thought he'd been pretty much right about that. There were still some hassles, still some like Jeremiah Cochran who'd never accept blacks as their neighbors, never mind equals, but it was hard to ignore the progress. The school was the most obvious place to see that. The new principal—Mrs. Lee everybody called her now—had been just Lettie when she and Albert were growing up together in the West End. Lettie was always the smartest kid in school, and that hadn't changed after consolidation. Now she was the boss. And the basketball coach, Barry Robinson, he'd been a star forward up in D.C. at Howard, and now in his fourth year as coach had earned the respect of all the players, and nearly all the parents.

Cochran didn't bother Albert. Live and let live, was his motto. The man just didn't know any better.

The cow was in the high pasture, so they all climbed into Cochran's truck, Sonny in the middle, Albert's bulk squeezed against the door, and drove up a gravel track off the county blacktop to a stock gate. The old man led the way through the field, steaming and cursing.

"Those damn kids," he muttered. "Damn no-good kids."

They found the cow, plump and peaceful, except for the buzzing horde of flies. By the time Albert discovered the makeshift camp, nosing around in the woods from the direction he guessed the shots had come, he knew for sure he was going to be late to DeShawn's game. He could have left Sonny out there to keep at it, but he saw Sonny had no idea what he was doing, that the man needed to be taught, just as much as anybody did starting out.

"Beer cans," Cochran said, pointing at the litter. "Maybe some, whatchacallums, fingerprints on those cans there."

Albert nodded, doubting his minuscule crime lab could do much with beer cans. But he had Sonny bag a couple anyway. Cigarette butts all over, fast food wrappers. Not much to go on.

"Lookee here," Sonny said, crouched at the edge of the camp. "Think we got us a clue." A jacket. A green, nylon, over-sized South River High School jacket, complete with initials.

With a call to his old friend Lettie, Albert matched the jacket to a boy at the high school. Freddy McDermott—football player, poor grades, cocky. A ringleader.

"Do you know him?" Albert asked DeShawn that night. He'd pulled the boy out to the porch with the high school yearbook while Sheryl bathed Juliette and put her to bed. DeShawn had barely spoken to him during supper. There'd been so many missed games in his freshman spring at South River High, and Albert had hoped the summer league would give him a chance to make it up to the boy. So far it wasn't turning out that way.

"This McDermott kid—you know him?"

DeShawn's arrival had come at a good time for Albert and Sheryl. After five years of marriage—both of them working hard to build for the future, Sheryl putting in long days as a nurse at the county hospital, and Albert climbing up from corrections officer to be one of a handful of deputies—they'd had a baby, a tiny thing they'd named Juliette. Considering that upheaval, adding DeShawn to the household had barely rocked the boat.

It wasn't exactly quiet on the porch, with a radio blaring from the community center and traffic whizzing along the street. Albert slapped at a mosquito on his neck.

"No, man. I mean, yeah, sure. Everybody knows him. But I don't *know* him, know what I mean? I don't, like, hang with him or nothing."

"Show me his picture, Dee."

DeShawn twisted his red ball-cap to the side and opened the heavy book to the juniors, ran his finger down the rows, turned a page, and tapped on a headshot. Albert couldn't tell much from that—a big white kid, blond hair buzzed short, fuzz on the chin. Like a lot of other boys.

"Who're his buddies? Any more pictures of him? What's he like?"

"Shit, man, why you asking all those questions? I told you, I don't know the dude. He's white, you know?" But DeShawn flipped through some more pages, found the football team, showed Albert a picture of Freddy McDermott in full regalia, doing blocking drills with another kid while the coaching staff looked on.

"Is he a troublemaker?"

"I don't know, man." DeShawn slammed the book shut and stalked into the house, let the screen door bang behind him. Upstairs, Juliette howled. Hip-hop boomed from the community center. Albert's head turned toward the smell of burgers on a grill nearby.

Sunday morning, Albert and Sonny drove out to the McDermott house, a low-slung double-wide next to a muddy pond off Chestnut Road. Bikes and basketballs littered the gravel drive, along with two pickups, one with "FREDDY" on the license plate. The patchy lawn smelled of skunkweed and wild onions. Sonny carried the jacket and followed Albert to the door. A low growl, like a far-off lawnmower, greeted them before they got close. Albert saw the mutt's tan muzzle pressed into the screen, and the gleaming, bared teeth. With one hand on his holstered gun, Albert raised the other to knock, and the dog let loose a tirade, leaped, and put his front paws through the screen. Sonny jumped back.

"Jesus," Sonny said.

"Rufus, you get down from there," shouted a woman's voice from inside. "Get down, you." A hand appeared from the shadows and yanked the stout dog by the collar before a whole body stepped into the picture—mousy curls, sweatshirt and bulging cutoffs, veiny white thighs.

"Excuse us, Ma'am," said Albert.

"You got my dog all bothered," said the woman.

"We're truly sorry, Ma'am. Might want to fix that screen, when you get a chance." The dog struggled against the woman's grip, and she stared at Albert, eyes narrowed into slits as if to say she wouldn't have a problem letting go of Rufus if she didn't like what she heard.

"Deputy Halliwell, Ma'am. This is Sonny Chambers. We're looking for Freddy."

The woman stepped back into the shadows, pulling Rufus with her. "Freddy," she yelled into the house, "Get your butt out here." Then nothing. Albert turned at the clanking of a truck passing too fast on the narrow road and looked back to see the woman still choking the dog. "Freddy," she shouted again.

"Why?" called a voice from the back, muffled, through a door. Then the boy appeared, pulling a gray t-shirt over his head and big shoulders. Barefoot, baggy shorts.

"You Freddy McDermott?"

"Yeah. What of it?" He was pressed against the torn screen now, like the mutt had been, and looked nearly as ready to pounce. But the boy eased back. Caught sight of the uniform, Albert knew—set his mind to racing.

"Come on out here, son."

The boy muttered, "Ain't your son," but pushed the door open and edged onto the stoop.

He was a massive kid, taller than Albert, built solid, but Albert still probably outweighed him some, big around the middle as he'd gotten.

"This yours?" Albert reached behind him and took the jacket out of Sonny's hands. "And don't tell me it's not, because I know it is."

"Sure, it's mine. Somebody steal it?"

"Well, now, that might be what happened." The boy reached out for the jacket. Albert pulled it away and handed it back to Sonny. "But I don't think so." Freddy blocked most of the door, but Albert could see the boy's mother in the shadows, peering out, holding the snarling dog. Albert nodded toward the drive and let the boy lead the way, out of his mother's earshot.

"What I think happened, Freddy, is that you lost this jacket when you and your pals were out in the woods drinking and maybe consuming something else that a drug test would likely confirm. And I also think you boys used a cow for target practice." Albert thought he saw the beginnings of a grin on Freddy's face, like he either thought shooting a cow was damn funny, or maybe he was relieved that the cow was the problem and he hadn't been caught doing something else he'd done that was probably far worse.

"Now you may think it's a joke, Freddy, but we got us a dead cow on our hands, and there's a good old farmer who wants somebody to pay."

"It's just a cow, man. What's the big deal?"

"So you admit you shot the man's cow?"

"Didn't say that, now did I?" The grin again. Sonny snickered.

"But you were there. If you didn't shoot her then who did?"

This time the boy kept his mouth shut, crossed his beefy arms over his chest, and stared back at Albert.

"All you got to do, Freddy, is pay for the cow. A few hundred bucks, you and your buddies, and the old man'll forget it happened."

Nothing from Freddy, just a widening grin. The boy spat at his feet.

"All right then, Freddy, a drug test—"

"You're that boy DeShawn's daddy, ain't you? Scrawny little nigger?"

Albert took a deep breath.

"Better get you some shoes on. You're coming with us." For the first time in a long time Albert felt threatened, as if the boy's hatred was personal, more than just ignorance. He gripped Freddy's wrist, ready to drag him over to the patrol car, when his arms snapped forward, catching Albert in the face and knocking him back into Sonny. Freddy took off running, behind the house, into the woods fast as a cat, barefoot and all. Sonny ran after him but pulled up short, wheezing—the boy had already disappeared. Albert heard laughter from inside the house. The dog growled and jumped at the broken screen door.

That afternoon, Albert was late for DeShawn's summer league game at Schoolhouse Park, in the stadium that the town fathers had squeezed between the football field and the armory. He'd have been on time, but after he and Sonny gave up on Freddy, they'd had to chase a drunk farmer halfway across the county, only catching him because where the Pike made that dogleg left out past the old mill the farmer and the truck did not, which landed farmer and truck both in a muddy ditch. Sorting that out took a while and it was already the third inning when Albert plopped down next to Sheryl in the stands.

"Did he know I wasn't here?" Albert let the baby grab his finger.

"Now why would he have any reason to think you weren't here, Bert? Just because you haven't been on time to a damn thing the boy's been involved with since he moved here, doesn't mean your promises are worthless to him."

"You're beautiful when you're sarcastic, girl," he said. At least that got a grin out of her. He wished it were that easy with DeShawn. Albert looked around the stands to see who was there, to see where trouble might come from if there was any, a habit he'd been in for a long time, and not just since he became a deputy sheriff. Mostly parents and little kids, some in uniform ready for the next game that afternoon. But up at the top of the stands, passing around something in a paper bag, were Freddy McDermott and his crew. He'd have to keep an eye on them, do something if they got rowdy. Probably just a matter of time.

DeShawn's team, the Cardinals, was at bat. A chubby kid—Albert had forgotten his name but knew his dad was a banker—leaned over the plate, bat rested on his shoulder. Albert could see the boy's grip was all wrong, his feet planted like he didn't ever intend to move. Sure enough, three times in a row, the ball whizzed past him before he could get the bat started. He didn't look too upset as he headed to his seat, danger past for another rotation. Albert looked around, didn't see the father. Next up was Evan something, a handsome boy with thick, dark hair, a solid build for a thirteen year old, and he set himself up over the plate like he just knew he was going to clobber the ball, and wanted the pitcher to know it, too. "Hit it Evan," a chorus shouted in the stands, the boy's whole family, Albert figured. He caught a glimpse of DeShawn then, halfway to the plate, warming up, swinging the bat. Albert waved, but maybe DeShawn had already given up on him, or maybe he was just concentrating, because he wasn't looking into the stands. Bat cracked against ball, Evan barreled up the line to first, rounded to second, and the crowd cheered for him to keep going. The centerfielder finally tracked down the ball and hurled it wildly, coming closest to the kid on first, who managed a rocket to third, but Evan slid under it in a dusty explosion. Safe!

DeShawn stepped to the plate, waited for the hubbub to settle, and took up his stance. Not bad, Albert thought, good crouch, grip looks tight but not too tight, good motion on the bat. He wanted to shout, to cheer the boy on and let him know he was there for him, but wouldn't it be awful if it made him look up into the stands just as a perfect pitch waffled by? Let the boy play. Albert leaned forward.

DeShawn watched the first pitch zoom past, a good strike. Where'd he learn to be so patient? I'd have been all over that one, Albert thought. The next pitch was high and outside, and DeShwan let that one go, too. Then a fastball, down the middle. DeShawn just stood there. Strike Two! Another one wide. And another one. It seemed like DeShawn was going to stand there all day, silent and immobile, like the top of some Little League trophy. The pitcher must have thought so, too. He wound up, let a fastball rip, and DeShawn swung at exactly the right instant. The ball sailed over the chain link fence in left field and rolled into the parking lot as Evan scored and DeShawn ran the bases, grinning, headed for home.

The crowd was on its feet and the ovation filled Albert with pride. DeShawn disappeared into a swarm of his teammates, all hugs and high-fives. Somebody patted Albert on the back, he didn't even know who. Sheryl squeezed his arm. He barely noticed the next two boys ground out to end the inning. The Cardinals trotted onto the field, to the shouts of a dozen or so sets of parents, a mix of white and black that comforted Albert. Even the Chens were there, maybe the only Asian family in the county, shouting for their son Troy, a lanky kid sprinting out to take up his spot in deep right. This is good, Albert thought. Real good.

"Where's Dee?" Albert stood and shaded his eyes. A couple of black kids fidgeted on the bench; one Albert recognized was Marcus Johnson, DeShawn's best friend, and the other was an awkward looking boy, tall, glasses, by himself at the end, staring into the dirt like he had no prospects of getting into the game. There was a white kid at shortstop, DeShawn's usual position, pale, freckled arms poking out of the red jersey, the bill of his cap pulled low. Jimmy something was on the mound, a big redhead, and Willie Burgess, another of Dee's buddies, looked nervous at first base. Around the horn and the outfield. No sign of DeShawn.

Albert kissed Sheryl and the baby and climbed past the Lewis family, Tom and Wendy and their pre-schooler, Jessica, Albert thought her name was. Tom was a volunteer fireman, and he and Albert had known each other a long time, but Tom had been cool to the idea of his boy, T.J., short for Tom Junior, hanging out with DeShawn, even though they were the same age and in the same classes in school. It was something Albert had planned on, Dee being friends with the son of his friend, but it hadn't happened. He hadn't understood it at the time, but maybe Tom wasn't much different from that boy, Freddy. Maybe they were all like that and Albert had just been blind. Tom nodded as Albert went by, kept his eyes on the game.

Albert crouched behind the team's bench. "Marcus! Hey Marcus, where's DeShawn?" Marcus jerked around, tottered on the edge of the bench.

"He's not here. I mean he was here. Did you see his home run? Man, that was something."

"Where's he now, Marcus?"

"Some guys started pushing him and he ran over behind the gym thing and—"

"The armory?" Marcus nodded. "Who? What guys?"

"Big white guy from school."

Albert looked up in the stands, saw the empty bleachers where Freddy McDermott and company had been. He jogged toward the armory, already wondering what he'd tell Aunt Denise, how DeShawn had come out here to get away from the violence and here, in this peaceful little town full of rednecks and white trash . . . He turned the corner, but there was no one. He ran the length of the building, turned again and nothing.

Sheryl was waiting for him by the Cherokee, Juliette in her arms. "Where's DeShawn?"

Albert was bent nearly double, catching his breath. "He's running from some kids. Stay here. No—go home. That's where he'd be headed." Albert jumped toward the patrol car just as the tall, awkward boy approached, eyes on the splintered asphalt.

"I saw 'em," the boy said.

"Saw who, son?" Albert grabbed him by the shoulders, tried to make the boy look up and into his eyes. "Who'd you see?"

"DeShawn. With them boys." He sniffed, as if he might be about to cry.

"Tell me where."

The boy's hand flapped toward the armory, then back to his side. "Over there. They started messing with us and one boy knocked me down and DeShawn pushed him back and told him to stop it and they grabbed him and kicked him and he told me to run." The boy pulled off his cap and twisted it in his hands. "That's the last I seen of 'em." A cheer rose from the stands and they both turned to look.

"You get on back now. I'll find DeShawn."

Wiping his nose on his sleeve, the boy shuffled back to his place on the bench.

Albert raced through town toward the McDermott trailer. When the traffic light at Skyview and Payne didn't go his way, he switched on the lights and siren, pulled around a beat-up Caprice and sped through the intersection, swerving to miss a head-phoned teenager in a Civic. He rounded the corner at Chestnut, tires squealing, and spun onto the gravel drive of the doublewide. Freddy's truck was gone. The dog was staked out front, snarling and snapping at Albert. He couldn't get past the dog even to knock on the door.

"Mrs. McDermott? You in there? Anybody home?" He could see through the torn screen that the front door was closed. He checked in back. The windows were open, but he heard nothing inside. Eyes on the dog, he climbed back in the patrol car. The radio crackled.

"Albert? Can you hear me? Pick up if you hear me!" It was Sonny's voice, unaccustomed still to police radio protocol.

"I hear you, Sonny. What's up?"

"It's old man Cochran. Says somebody's in the woods shooting things up again."

Should've known, Albert thought. "Tell Mr. Cochran I'm on my way."

The old man drove Albert up to where they'd found the cow. Freddy's truck sat just at the edge of the pasture. A shot sent a trio of crows into the sky and echoed back across the hollow.

"That's a shotgun," Albert said. He pulled his pistol, told Cochran to stay put, and ran to Freddy's pickup. He heard laughter, three voices at least, heard somebody say, "Hey, Freddy, toss me one." A can fizzed open. He reached into the truck, tugged the keys out of the ignition and edged through the woods toward the voices.

The boys were in the clearing where Albert and Sonny had found the jacket. Four kids, not three, all big, like Freddy. Freddy sat on a log with another boy, drinking beer. A third stood on the perimeter, pissing against a tree, and the fourth, a tall kid with a dark buzz cut, stood with his back to Albert, aiming the shotgun at a row of beer cans set up on a stump, twenty-five yards away. And there was DeShawn, back against a tree just outside the clearing, gagged, head drooped, hands and feet tied.

"Put that gun down," Albert blurted, his voice shaking. He aimed at the dark-haired boy and stepped into the clearing, watching the others out of the corner of his eye. "Now!"

The kid turned with the shotgun still braced against his shoulder and Albert slid back behind a tree.

"Jesus, don't shoot," said the boy. He lowered the gun, knelt, set it on the ground, and held his hands up. The other boys dropped their beers and stood. Albert moved away from the tree and swung the pistol toward Freddy.

"Shit," said Freddy.

"Dee!" Albert saw the boy's head lift, look at him like he was miles away. "You okay?" DeShawn nodded. Albert moved forward then, faster than Freddy retreated. Freddy fell over a log and sprawled onto his back. Albert held the gun steady, aimed at Freddy's chest.

"Fuck! You can't just shoot me. I didn't do nothing."

The boy who'd held the shotgun took a step toward Albert, and Albert swung the pistol in his direction.

The boy stepped back. "Didn't mean no harm, man. Just having some fun with the kid."

"Shut up, Jake," shouted Freddy, struggling to get up. Albert drove his heel into Freddy's chest, knocking him flat.

"It was Freddy grabbed him from the ball field and we brought him out here to scare him. He was scared all right. Fast little bugger, too. Took us awhile to catch and rope him like that."

"Jake, you idiot, shut up."

"Jake," Albert said, eyes trained on Freddy again, "nice and slow now, you go on over to my boy and untie him. And Jake? You do anything stupid, I blow your friend's head off."

Jake did as he was told, loosened the gag and untied the rope around DeShawn's ankles, then the wrists. Albert thought he heard the kid whisper, "I'm sorry," to DeShawn. Jake lifted DeShawn to his feet.

DeShawn ran to Albert and put his arms around him, sobbing into his belly.

"Dee, you hurry down to see Mr. Cochran. Have him take you home, hear? Tell Sheryl I'll be there shortly." DeShawn edged backward, eyes shifting from Albert to the older boys and back, and when he came to the edge of the clearing he turned and sprinted through the trees.

"Thank you, Jake," Albert said. When he heard the growl of Cochran's truck fade toward town, he tossed Freddy's keys to Jake and pointed to the other two boys. "Y'all head on home now. And I don't want any more trouble from any of you. Ever. Now leave me with Freddy."

"Yessir," all three muttered, nearly tripping over themselves to get away, even as Freddy shouted for them to come back. Albert let their whoops and hollers and the rattle of Freddy's truck disappear. Freddy stopped his yelling, and the color drained from his face. Albert stared at Freddy, watched beads of sweat appear on his forehead.

The silence weighed on Albert. Like his silence all along, all those years. He couldn't ignore it anymore.

"It's just us now, boy," he said to Freddy. "Guess your buddies had something better to do." Freddy gazed in the direction of his departed friends. "Look at me when I'm talking to you, boy." Albert kicked Freddy, hard, between his legs. The boy groaned and curled in on himself.

"You son of a bitch, look at me." Albert lifted the gun, aimed it at the boy's face.

Freddy rolled over, whimpering like a dog. "You stupid nigger."

It's not the way I always pretended it was, Albert thought. They haven't changed at all.

"I think I need some target practice, boy." Albert kicked Freddy again. "Isn't every day I get to shoot a fine young redneck like yourself. Wouldn't want to miss." He spun around and fired. A tin can on the log pinged away. He turned back, held the gun close to Freddy's nose so he'd smell the burn. Albert could see the boy's whole body tremble. Why did I think we'd made progress? Because of a few teachers? Because they gave me a gun?

"I'll tell folks how you tried to grab my gun while I was putting the cuffs on you," Albert said. "How it went off in the struggle. One less bigot. World's a better place."

"Jesus," said Freddy, choking back sobs. "Nobody'll believe that."

"I've got the badge, boy. They'll believe."

"Jesus, man, don't shoot."

Albert stepped back, eyes on Freddy's quivering face, raised the gun again, aimed at the middle of the boy's forehead. He thought of his father's life of menial jobs, and his mother cleaning up after white people. He thought of the hell DeShawn had come from and everything he'd been through at the hands of this boy, and he wanted to make this boy pay.

"Guess I don't need no more practice," Albert said.

"Jesus!" Freddy squeezed his eyes shut.

Albert thought about Jeremiah Cochran and Sonny Chambers and all those men who looked at Albert like he wasn't there. He thought about how hard it was for people like Lettie Lee and Barry Robinson to rise up, and these people just didn't understand. Freddy McDermott had to learn what it meant to suffer. They all had to learn.

Albert held the gun steady, shifted the barrel a tick left of the boy's head, and fired.

STONEWALL

Willard Spencer's eyes drifted shut as the news droned on—some hoarse general certain coalition forces were closing in on Saddam, some nameless private wasted by a suicide bomb in Fallujah. Willard had heard it all before, in this war and the last. Wasn't that much different when he served in Vietnam, just the color of the bastards they were fighting, and the damn government's excuses. His eyes jerked open when the banging on his front door started, explosive and insistent.

He dragged himself to the door, wondering why the dogs weren't raising a fuss. When they were on their game, they'd let him know the instant they picked up a strange scent, best home security system to be had. Better late than never, the animals came to life, Stonewall first and loudest.

The deadbolt rattled from the pounding.

"All right already," he called. "Hold your horses." He pulled the door open and there was Fred Givens, in a rain-soaked cap, hands on his hips, face red as a beefsteak tomato. Bugs pinged around the porch light. Fred circled the stoop like a hound in a cage.

"You want to use the bathroom, Fred?" Willard held the door, but Fred made no move to come in. His truck sat in the driveway, high beams aimed at the garage door, motor hacking. Rain spilled out of Willard's clogged gutters and pelted the muddy walk.

"What I want, you son-of-a-bitch, is for you to stay away from my goddamn wife." Fred slapped the porch railing and both men watched it shake.

Willard stepped out, batted a moth from his ear. "Don't know what you're yakking about, Fred." It was a stall he'd used often enough with Jenny, although his ex-wife had stopped buying it early on. When she got a notion stuck in her craw, like he'd dipped into their savings for poker stakes, or had his eye on a waitress at Rocky's Tavern, she wouldn't quit. Still, no point giving anything away too soon, even if Fred was off base.

"You know damn well what I mean, Willard."

"Is Ellie with you?" Willard peered into the truck.

"Just stay away from her. Or you'll regret it. You hear me?"

The dogs' whimpering struck up at dawn. At least that's when Willard was awake to it. The noise got louder as gray light filtered into his stuffy bedroom. He reached to the nightstand for his cigarettes and, finding none, remembered that he'd quit. Six months since the chest pains started, six months since Doc Malone spelled it all out. Quit or die. Would the wanting ever stop?

Not that he was desperate. He kept the hunger in check, felt it climb up his throat now and again, but always managed to fight it back. Not like some folks he knew, like his own brother Dickie, who'd let his cravings push him around. Dickie was out of control. It wasn't the cancer that drove him to pull the trigger.

Willard tugged on a t-shirt, snug over his age-swollen belly. Jeans were tight, too, belt on the last hole. Might have to punch a new one, he thought, and ran his finger past the buckle to measure how much room was left. Maybe he'd spring for a bigger size at the Wal-Mart, give in to this one side of being sixty. It wasn't as if anybody cared what he looked like. Nobody'd ever cared, not even Jenny, and their marriage lasted thirty years. Wasn't his looks that drove her off, Willard was reasonably sure. At least that never came up when she was screaming at him about chasing women, having no money, and tracking dirt into the house. He noticed the mud on his boots, cursed himself for not leaving them outside when he came in the night before, and thought about carrying them to the porch. He shrugged and laced them on. Grassy clods fell to the pine floor and shattered.

The whimpering was even louder now—mixed with muffled yips and yelps—and Stonewall, the old golden retriever, taking charge as he did every morning, started to bark.

"I'm coming," yelled Willard. He pushed out the back door, and now that they could see him, all the dogs let loose: Mosby's howl, high-pitched for a shepherd, Jeb's deep-throated rottweiler cough, Stonewall's hungry shout, and Dickie's twin cockers, Daisy and Clover, with their anxious yapping and pacing inside the chain-link kennel, nails tapping on the cement floor.

Dawn haze lapped at the looming Blue Ridge like waves on the shore. Behind him, fog crept out of the pine woods and over the rolling ex-battlefield. In weather like that it wasn't hard to conjure campfires and cannon, a white-tent city stretching across the pasture where now Randy Bell's doleful Black Angus herd grazed.

Willard unlocked the shed before opening the kennels. Some sleepy mornings he'd forget, and the dogs'd nearly knock him over as he dished up their chow. Easier to let them bark in the pens, no matter how edgy it made him. Their mouths would be occupied soon enough, and there'd be peace for about a minute. He took the lid off the garbage pail that held the kibble, scooped out enough for the gang, and sealed it up again. He filled three bowls and then opened one of the two kennels to let the boys out. Silenced, the dogs pushed past him with Stonewall, reddish gold and sleek, in the lead. Daisy and Clover still paced, but quietly, eyes fixed on him, long pink tongues slapping their jaws. He fed them inside their kennel, to make sure the boys didn't claim more than their share.

"Enjoy your breakfast, girls," Willard said. Dickie had always called them "the girls."

Ellie's Grand Cherokee pulled into the drive. Daisy looked up from her bowl briefly, but the rest paid no mind. Willard slipped into the house and met her on the porch.

"He was here," Willard said, his voice low. The nearest house was a quarter-mile away, but Willard swept his gaze along the road. He remembered the shouting match he and Jenny had in the yard one evening and the visit from the Sheriff, thanks to a neighbor's vigilance. Miz Doak didn't miss a trick.

"I figured as much," Ellie said. "He came home last night ranting and raving. Wouldn't listen to a thing I said—not that that's anything new."

"Maybe we should give him something to worry about." He thought he saw Ellie blush. "High school was a long time ago."

"A very long time ago."

"What brings you this way, Ellie?"

"Just . . . he has a gun, you know."

"Everybody's got a goddamn gun."

Willard didn't know what to make of Ellie's visit. They'd gone out as kids, back before he met Jenny, just sodas at the Ice Dream and maybe a drive-in movie with as much heavy-breathing as kids did in those days. Fred wasn't in the picture then, either. But Ellie'd never been to the house before now, at least not since Jenny took off and made him a free man. Not that he minded the visit. He used to run into Fred and Ellie at the Elks from time to time, and one lonely night about a year back, after a tongue-tied phone call—he and Jenny were already on the outs by then and heading downhill—he'd convinced Ellie to meet him for beers at Rocky's Tavern. They talked about old times. He'd been hoping their youthful attraction might rekindle, and he sure didn't give a damn about Fred Givens. He told her as much, but Ellie'd got cold feet after the second drink.

"I'm no good at this," she'd said.

"Hell, girl, we haven't done anything yet," Willard had replied.

But she'd let out a sigh, pecked him on the cheek, pulled car keys from her purse, and headed home.

A letter came from Jenny demanding money, said he owed her that much after all she'd put up with. Not that she was wrong. He wasn't perfect. He had faults same as any man. But he'd always worked hard. Wasn't that enough? Wasn't she the one who walked out?

He fed the dogs again at dusk before he left for bowling. The league had been something he and Dickie did together, even though Willard had never liked it much, and each time up was just as likely to roll a gutter ball as a strike. Still, he'd kept going on his own this past year. Force of habit, he told himself, but he knew it might be more than that. It had been important to Dickie, and he'd won bowler-of-the-year more than once. At least there was that one thing his brother could be proud of. Willard couldn't remember if he'd ever congratulated Dickie for those trophies.

Ellie was at the bowling alley, at the far lane, with a bunch of women doing more laughing and talking than bowling. He'd never seen her there before, but he'd mentioned the league that morning when she stopped by. He hadn't meant anything by it; it was just conversation. But now he was glad she'd come. She glanced his way a few times.

Between games he drank a Rolling Rock at the bar. He watched Ellie come toward him, her full hips swaying, the gold hoops of her earrings bouncing to the same rhythm. She ordered a Bud and stood next to him. She smelled of lilacs.

"Fancy meeting you here," she said, not looking at Willard. The crack of ball against pins echoed in the lounge, followed by cheers.

"Quite a coincidence." He noticed the glossy red of her lips and nails, the tight curls in her hair.

"I was thinking about what you said this morning." She sipped her beer.

He wasn't sure what she meant. He wondered if she had a cigarette.

"Fred isn't so easy to live with, you know." Now she looked at him. "It's been hard lately."

"He's a moron, Ellie." He fixed his eyes on hers. "A moron who doesn't know when he's got it good."

That night, Willard couldn't sleep. Stonewall wouldn't keep his mouth shut—a skunk, or a coon, probably, but there wasn't anything Willard could do about it—and on top of that there was worry over the letter from Jenny. Where did she think he'd put his hands on any money? As it was, he didn't know how he'd manage. The auto parts business was as slow as he could remember. He should have sold out when he had the chance; probably it was too late now. He was still paying off Dickie's bills. And he couldn't get Ellie off his mind, or Fred's threats. He put on his robe and slippers and shuffled out to the porch.

"Stonewall Jackson, shut the fuck up," he shouted, and the dog stopped barking, only until Willard was back in bed.

He threw back the sheet and pulled on his jeans, stumbling when he lost his balance. He banged his toe on the dresser and cursed. He snatched up the t-shirt he'd flung on the floor and wrestled that on. He found yesterday's socks balled under the bureau. His foot throbbed, his toe surely broken. He couldn't find his boots and then remembered he'd left them on the porch for once. He looked in the nightstand for cigarettes and found none, but grabbed his .45 from the drawer. If there was a coon, maybe he could shoot it.

All the dogs launched into a barking frenzy when they saw him running out with his flashlight. "Shut up," he yelled. "Just shut up, you goddamn dogs." Stonewall wouldn't stop—his bark was loud, vehement. Willard stormed to the kennels, unlocked Stonewall's and pushed Jeb and Mosby back. Stonewall zipped out, galloped around the yard twice, his dense, blond tail flying, then came back, rubbing his snout against Willard's leg. He crouched at Willard's feet and gazed up at him, still barking. Willard grabbed him by the scruff, yanked him away from the chain link. Stonewall yelped, but Willard didn't stop. He yanked again. "Shut-the-god-damn-fuck-up," Willard said, tightening his grip and raising his voice with each word, his whole body trembling, his heart racing. Stonewall snarled and tried to pull away, bared his teeth and snapped. Blood oozed from the punctures in Willard's hand.

Without thinking, chuffing through his nostrils, his jaw clamped, chest pounding, he fumbled at the waist of his jeans for the pistol, put the barrel to the dog's head, and fired.

Stonewall dropped. The shot echoed between house and hills. The other dogs fell quiet.

Willard still clutched the gun. He stared down at Stonewall, surprised by his stillness. How could the dog be so still? Maybe there was movement, a twitch? Was it too late to undo what he'd done? He dropped the gun and knelt by the dog's body. His hands shook. He touched Stonewall's shoulder, first with one finger, then two. Why didn't he move? He sat in the grass and stroked the dog's flank. He could scarcely look at the head, the black gash where the ear had been, the dark blood matting the golden hair. Willard wiped the sweat from his face. His breath came hard.

"You should've listened to me," he whispered.

In the morning, Willard picked up the phone. He hadn't planned the call. It just came to him while he drank coffee on the porch—struggling to wake up after the ruinous night, conscious of his bandaged, throbbing hand and the still-aching toe. He watched the dogs mope around the yard, as if looking for Stonewall, confused by his absence and the smell of blood. Daisy and Clover huddled together; Mosby and Jeb sniffed each other and circled close. Willard needed to do something about Stonewall, as if that would assure the dogs it wouldn't happen again. He called the sheriff.

Deputy Albert Halliwell stopped by the house in the evening, while Willard was hosing down the yard. Willard had known Albert for years, had sold him a head gasket at the store for his wife's Honda and helped him install it. He seemed like a good man, and Willard figured he had it rough as the only black deputy the county had ever hired, someone Willard could count on, someone who knew who his friends were. Willard stuck his bandaged hand in his pocket.

"We don't usually take missing dog reports, Willard," Albert said. "You put an ad in?"

Willard shook his head. "Suspected something is all. That Fred Givens came around here waving a gun and making threats."

"About the dog?" Albert asked.

"About his wife."

Albert stared at Willard. "That's a serious thing. You accusing him?"

"He knows better than to mess with me. But an animal—that's a different story."

Albert wrote it all down, how Willard checked on the dogs when he came home from bowling but couldn't swear they were all there—it was dark and he'd had a beer or two at the lanes. With so many legs and snouts jumping and yapping, how could you tell? So he didn't notice anything wrong until he went to feed them that morning.

"Strangest thing. Normally they start a ruckus at sunup and kick into another gear altogether when I come out. But they were quiet as mice. You just knew something was wrong. And Stonewall nowhere to be seen." Willard had checked the fences, he said, and saw no sign that Stonewall had dug out. "And even if he'd run off somewhere, he'd be back for breakfast. That dog's never missed a meal in his life."

Next evening, with the last light fading over the ex-battlefield, Willard went out to the shed. The dogs eyed him warily. Willard thought he heard the cockers whine, but they hushed when he looked their way. He slipped the key in the padlock, opened the double doors, and peered into the shadows. A cardinal whistled in the woods and he turned to look, but there was nothing to see. He knelt, lifted the tarp off Stonewall's body, and draped it over the lawn tractor. The dog's eyes stared.

Willard cradled the body and carried it to the side of the house, kicked the gate open, and knelt again to lay Stonewall gently on the gravel drive. He poured engine oil on the blood in the shed and covered it with sawdust. Then Willard called Albert and sat on the porch to wait. The sky turned gray, then black.

When Albert pulled in the driveway, the patrol car's lights washed over Stonewall. Willard turned away.

"That him?" Albert raised one foot to the porch, a flashlight in his hand.

"Son-of-a-bitch killed him. Found him lying in a ditch."

"Hit by a car probably," said Albert as they crossed the drive. He trained the light on the body.

"Shot in the head, plain as day," said Willard. "And that son-of-a-bitch was the one that shot him. Now what are you going to do about it?"

Willard knelt by Stonewall and stroked him. Albert kept the flashlight high—the circle of light tied together the fence, the corner of the house, the squad car fender. Willard loosened Stonewall's bloodied collar and pulled it over the dog's head. He closed his hand around the tags to stop their jangling. Mosby and Jeb barked from the kennel.

On Saturday afternoon, Willard's doorbell rang. He recognized the kids from the ramshackle house down the road. Their folks were Roy and Nell—that much he knew. He thought the girl's name might be Rosemary—Jenny had mentioned her once or twice—but he drew a blank on the boy. He reached for his wallet to buy whatever it was they were selling.

"What've you got?" He figured it wasn't Girl Scout cookies, or the boy wouldn't be there. Probably candy for school, or magazines. He liked to help out when he could since he and Jenny never had kids. And Dickie's wife had taken their boy away after the divorce. Willard hadn't seen him in years. They hadn't even come to the funeral.

The girl wrinkled her nose.

"We're sorry about your dog," said the boy. "Mrs. Spencer used to let us play with him sometimes."

"He was a real nice dog," said the girl. Willard put his wallet away.

Albert called to tell him they'd had the vet look at the body, since Willard was claiming a crime had been committed. They didn't normally do autopsies on dogs. Stonewall died of a bullet to the head—a bullet that killed him instantly, passed right through his brain and was gone.

"I told you who did it, Albert. You ought to arrest that Fred Givens."

"Fred says he didn't do it, Willard."

"And I suppose you believe him. What about those threats?"

"Got no way to prove it. It's just your word, and you said yourself you didn't see it. We could search for the bullet if you'll show us where you found him."

Two younger deputies came to the house, and Willard rode with them a half-mile up the road to where he said he'd found Stonewall. He folded his arms across his chest and watched while the deputies combed the ditch. They ripped out the wild rose bushes and tangled creeper, and filled a garbage sack with beer bottles and Coke cans. They dug right down to the dirt, but found no bullet, or blood.

"Don't mean nothing," said one of the deputies. "Dumped him here afterwards, more'n likely."

Next morning, with just a hint of light through the trees, Willard got the newspaper out of the box. The dogs yapped as usual, back to their old ways, but he felt like making them wait. Seemed the dogs never learned a damn thing. They saw what happened to Stonewall, but there they were, still fussing. He missed the old boy, best dog he'd ever had. Should've been Jenny's favorite, Jeb. Or one of Dickie's nervous mutts. He gave in and fed the dogs, then settled down to the paper. He craved a cigarette, patted his shirt pocket the way he used to, but it was empty. He eyed the kitchen drawers where Jenny had kept the cartons he brought home from the wholesale store, but he knew they were empty too, or anyway they were filled now with junk—pencils, an old padlock he hadn't wanted to waste, Stonewall's tags.

Willard opened the paper and saw a picture of Stonewall, tongue hanging out the side of his mouth. How the hell did they get a picture? It was a snapshot Jenny had taken. Did she have something to do with it? If she wanted out of his life so bad, why couldn't she mind her own business? There was Willard's knee just to the right of the dog's head, and Dickie's boy was a blur in the background. The article was about animal cruelty. The Sheriff had heard complaints over the past few months about a murdered cow, a widow with a slew of sick cats in her basement, and now the killing of Stonewall. No bullet had been found, the article said, but there was a suspect. The SPCA demanded stiff penalties. Various downtown shoppers had been asked their opinions—everyone said the killer should be thrown in jail.

"Who would shoot a poor dog?" asked one woman. "People who hurt animals are no better than animals themselves. Lock him up, I say."

Willard drank his coffee. He hadn't counted on publicity. He'd lost his temper, was all, under a lot of pressure, and he was mad at Fred for what he'd said about him and Ellie. It all seemed to fit, like pieces of those jigsaw puzzles he and Dickie worked as kids. The story just jumped out from the mess. But he hadn't meant for the whole town to know. He spilled coffee when he set the mug down and let it soak into the paper.

He worked in the yard. He spent most of the morning trying to find the bullet. Albert had said it had passed through Stonewall's skull, so it must have lodged in the dirt somewhere. Willard got down on his hands and knees, searching the grass with his fingers while the dogs watched silently from the kennel. Nothing. He gave up and moved on to the shed, sweeping up the sawdust mixed with blood and oil, leaving a pear-shaped stain. He heard the phone ringing in the house. He let it ring. Was there any way to tell what left the stain? Back on his knees, he scoured the floor with laundry soap and a brush. Then he soaked the floor with bleach.

In the afternoon, his doorbell rang. The reporter who'd written the newspaper story needed to ask him a few questions. The paper had been flooded with calls from readers wanting to know what the Sheriff was doing about the crime. Willard tried to answer, but his mouth was dry and he felt short of breath. His phone was ringing again. Two cars and a pickup truck crawled by the house and the drivers' heads turned to look at him. Albert's squad car pulled in and stopped beside the reporter's Toyota. Willard patted his shirt pocket for the phantom cigarettes.

The reporter was a young woman. Her hair was dark and short, mannish, Willard thought. He told her exactly what he'd told Albert, as Albert walked up the drive. Had he left anything out? It always worked that way, it seemed. You forget, when you make something up, that you might have to repeat it. How easy to slip and get caught. Didn't he learn that lesson as a boy, lying to his mother about skipping school, and catching hell when the details didn't match what he told his father? Dickie had always believed whatever tales Willard told, but what about when he'd mixed himself up telling Jenny about working late, when he was really down at Rocky's?

"Who did this, Mr. Spencer?" asked the reporter. Her pen was poised over a notepad. Albert watched Willard and the reporter from the bottom of the steps.

"Don't know, Miss. But me, I'd talk to an old bastard name of Fred Givens." He should stop digging that hole, Willard thought, too late. Let things settle.

"Now you've done it," said Albert when the reporter was gone. "Fred's name'll be all over town by dark."

"You here to say you've arrested him?"

"I'm here because you don't answer your phone. I'm supposed to tell you the county supervisors are holding a special meeting on animal cruelty Monday night. They'd like it if you would kindly attend and tell about your dog."

At the meeting, in the airless courthouse, Supervisor Powell banged his gavel and stood up, facing a standing-room crowd. The women fanned themselves with whatever they could find in their purses. The men squirmed.

"Folks, I guess we all know why we're here," Powell said. "Let's hear what Willard Spencer has to say. Willard?"

That caught Willard off guard. He'd been late and hoped he'd be unnoticed in back, but Albert saw him and shepherded him to the front row. He scanned the room. Ellie was on the opposite side. He didn't see Fred.

He stood and told his story. He'd rehearsed it over the weekend and on the drive into town, and he was sure it was the same as he'd told Albert and that reporter. He reminded himself to stick to a few details—Fred's threats, finding his old friend with a bullet through his head. Getting fancy would undo him. His voice shook at first, and he stumbled over his words, but then he thought about poor Stonewall and the story flowed.

After he finished, a woman with tears in her eyes raised her hand. Powell pointed at her with the gavel and she stood, tugging at a silver cross on a chain and pushing down her skirt, which had ridden up on her wide hips.

"I'm Carol Waters and I think it's terrible what happened to that poor dog," she said. "If the Sheriff isn't going to do anything about this, then I say we go after the man who did it." Shouts echoed her plea. Powell pounded his gavel.

Willard wondered how he could stop a mob from tearing Fred to pieces. It was a mistake to give the reporter Fred's name. The whole thing was a mistake.

"You better arrest the son-of-a-gun," yelled a man's voice from the rear. More cheers. Somebody turned loose a collie who wore a sandwich board over its back. "Save Me—Arrest the Killer," it said. The crowd laughed. Powell pounded the gavel again.

Fred Givens barreled into the room and marched to the front. Albert grabbed his elbow but Fred brushed him off. The crowd came to its feet as Fred faced Willard.

"I did not kill your damned dog," shouted Fred.

"Like hell," Willard said. Fred had always been a mean bastard. Folks would have no trouble believing he'd done this, no matter how loud he protested.

"Arrest him," said Carol Waters.

"Yeah, arrest him," shouted the man in back.

Fred took a swing at Willard that Willard barely dodged. Albert and another deputy snagged Fred from behind and pulled him from the room to cheers and applause and Fred's cursing. The meeting broke up and a crowd gathered around Willard to express condolences.

Willard watched the TV news that night. His reception of the local station was weak, but he saw a report of the fracas. Fred hadn't helped his case any by throwing that punch. He'd been charged with a misdemeanor, and that satisfied some folks, but already there was a clamor to upgrade to a felony. That would mean jail time. And since it turned out Fred had a record Willard hadn't known about—assault, involving Ellie, apparently, and a youthful robbery— he could get a stiff sentence, if it came to that. Maybe it was time to come clean, or at least admit there was no real proof of anything. Did he really want to do this to Fred? He heard a tap at his door that he thought was wind. He heard the tap again.

As he let Ellie in, he peered into the darkness behind her. The road was black and quiet.

"He's mad as a snake, Willard," Ellie said. She leaned against the kitchen counter while Willard rooted in the fridge. He pulled out two cans of Bud. "He can't understand why people have turned against him."

"He's a dog-killer, that's why."

"Is he?" She sipped her beer and surveyed Willard's kitchen. The dogs barked out back. "Because even to me he claims he's innocent. Normally when he does something boneheaded, he tells me right away. Brags about it, even."

Willard gulped his beer, patted his pockets.

"But I'm probably wrong." She touched Willard's arm; her hand lingered. "In fact, now that I think about it, he did say something about clubbing Stonewall to teach you a lesson. I thought maybe I should tell the Sheriff."

Willard took a drink and eyed her over the can. "Shot," he said.

"Right. A shotgun, he told me." She set her beer on the counter and put her arms around Willard.

"Pistol." Willard took a deep breath. He smelled lilacs in Ellie's hair.

"Yes, that's it. In his chest." She laid her head on Willard's shoulder.

"Head." Willard caressed her arm. "And he left the body in a ditch about a half-mile from here."

"Head," she said. "A half-mile. Of course."

RED PEONY

T hat's a 'blue crackling coconut,'" Tim said, after a cobalt explosion filled the night with white sparks popping above their heads like machine-gun fire.

Teddy felt Emily cringe in his arms. They leaned back in tandem on their picnic blanket and surveyed the smoke-filled sky, while Tim, nearby on his own blanket, applauded and cheered. For reasons Teddy had never understood, his younger brother was a fireworks nut. When they were kids, he'd been timid in everything else—terrified of the dark, afraid of snakes and stray dogs, wary of Snowflake, the barnyard goose—but in the execution of the family's Fourth of July celebrations and other miscellaneous gatherings on the farm that provided an excuse for big bangs and pyrotechnics, Tim was both fearless and knowledgeable. Even tonight, on a hot, dry holiday evening among a throng of strangers in Ruggles Park, when Tim was a mere spectator and not the designated incendiary, he was full of wisdom.

A new blast was followed by bright clusters that drifted on the breeze. "That one's 'red falling leaves.' Remember, Teddy?"

Teddy remembered summer nights by the farm pond, the family ensconced in rickety lawn chairs, swatting mosquitoes while Tim and their father used smoldering punk to light the fuse, run for cover, and then wait for the whistling launch and aerial boom, the oohs and ahs from their mother and grandfather. Tim had jumped and laughed and clapped every time. Teddy went along because it

173

was tradition, for their family and most families they knew. But each time the countdown to liftoff began he'd covered his ears and was sure it would end in disaster: calamitous burns, scorched fields, lost eyes.

He wanted to tell Emily about those days, wanted her to understand how different they'd been as boys, even though he hadn't realized it himself until now.

"That was one of my favorites," Tim said, as the red light-trail faded. "God's firecrackers." He laughed and looked back at Teddy, then up at the sky.

God again. Tim had talked about God a lot lately: at Christmas, when they'd both been home and learned about their father's illness; the chilly weekend in April he'd helped Teddy and Emily move to the farm from Richmond; at their father's funeral last month and Uncle Marvin's the month before that; the last few days when Tim had come out from D.C. to help rummage through their father's things. Emily's pregnancy was a gift from God, he'd said. Their father's death was God's will. Teddy hardly knew him any more.

Not that they'd ever had much in common, now that he thought about it, and it wasn't just Tim's love of fireworks or being gay. Tim had always been into music—listening to it, playing it—and discovered early on he had some skill on the guitar. Music never interested Teddy. On the other hand, Teddy liked to argue, presaging his route to a law practice, while Tim, younger, smaller, artistic, preferred at all cost to avoid confrontation.

Looking back on their childhood, Teddy marveled that he never saw it before, but now it seemed so plain that they weren't really brothers. And he wondered if Tim saw it, too.

What were they celebrating? So much about this year felt wrong, and for Teddy the fireworks didn't fit. He had weighty decisions to make. At Christmas he'd known he wouldn't take the job his firm had offered in California, despite the big money and prestige. He'd known he'd bring Emily here to have the baby, to be closer to his father, to live a quieter life and to carry on the centuries-old Callison family tradition in the valley. He'd land a spot in a small-town law practice, do real legal work for real people—wills and trusts, house closings—help his dad on the farm as best he could. But with his father gone? What would they do about the house now? The farm? He couldn't run it by himself. That wasn't him. And Emily said she was willing, but she'd never lived on a farm before. Would Tim come back to help? No way.

Another explosion. Now Tim narrated a 'silver chrysanthemum,' with its dense light, like a white sun, followed by a 'golden willow' and streamers that burned in the eye long after the flames had faded. Emily burrowed into Teddy's arms, lifted his hands onto her swollen belly. He felt the baby move just as a rocket exploded above them. Emily jumped and they laughed together; Tim looked at them and smiled, seemed eager to join in but wasn't part of the joke. Teddy wanted to tell him what had just happened—he'd always told Tim everything, even though Tim didn't reciprocate and for the longest time thought his sexuality was still secret—but he also wanted to keep something just between him and Emily. Tim didn't need to know everything.

Emily pointed, with only a slight elevation of her hand, a half-extended finger, toward another pregnant woman, a girl really, with wild red hair, also in the arms of a man, a boy, with swirling tattoos on both arms and his neck. The girl looked up just then and Emily half waved. The girl looked familiar. She smiled, lowered her head.

"You know her?" Teddy asked.

"She's about eight months from the look of her. Just like me."

"She's nothing like you." The girl's hair was nearly pink. She had none of Emily's style, none of her grace. A child. Too young.

He remembered where he'd seen her. At Christmas, in the gift shop, she sold them that glass ornament his dad picked out, the hand-painted angel. He'd watched her wrap the delicate bulb, fearing that it would slip from her fingers and shatter.

Tim opened his mouth as if to speak, but turned his attention back to the sky. Teddy suspected there was something bothering him. He hadn't mentioned his boyfriend once since he arrived.

Gareth had come with him for the funeral, but even then Teddy sensed a strain between them. Maybe it had just been the pressure of being together in a small, conservative community, not wanting their couple-ness to intrude on the somber occasion. Or maybe Gareth had felt he had nothing to contribute since he'd never met their father. But it seemed more than that. Tim and Gareth had stood apart, hadn't spoken, even afterwards at the house when visitors besieged the family, and Teddy couldn't help but wonder.

He'd tried to ask Tim about it this week, but got platitudes in response: "It's all part of the plan," and "Everything happens for a reason." Teddy had done a poor job of hiding his bemusement at Tim's sudden fatalism, and that only made Tim more sullen.

Another family had sprawled on their patch of lawn, just down the gentle slope: a couple with their toddler, an Asian kid. Korean? Chinese? Teddy couldn't tell the difference, but either way he guessed the girl was adopted. One of the partners in his firm in Richmond had adopted from China. But that was Richmond, another world. A tolerant world. He resolved to learn more about adoption law for his practice. If they were going to stay.

"That's a 'flaming palm,'" Tim said, and the sky was bright with the fronds of the fiery tree.

"How do they do that?" Teddy asked. He wasn't just humoring Tim. He really wanted to know. How could anyone build something like that and know how it was going to come out?

"As in life," Tim said, winking at Emily, "the secret's in the stuffing."

Before Tim came out from D.C. to help, Teddy and Emily had begun the process of wading through his father's things—his mother's, too, since it turned out her life had long ago been packed away in boxes. Teddy had pulled carton after carton out of the attic and soon his dad's room, the room that had been Teddy and Tim's growing up, was filled.

One box held photo albums and loose pictures that had either never made their way into the book or had worked their way free.

He could pick out himself as a kid, and Tim, and his dad, with strands of thin gray hair and his customary overalls. His mother, too, but she looked so young in the pictures, he wasn't as sure. She'd been gone so long. He tried to remember, but the image of her he conjured was distorted, as if through thick glass. His grandparents were in the pictures, too. He was just seven or eight when his grandmother died, the year of the flood. He barely remembered her, just fleeting smells, the dank earth of her skin, the spun sugar of her hair. Aunt Irene he could identify because of the pinched, disapproving expression on her face, portly Uncle Marvin at her side. And then there were older pictures: men and women he truly did not recognize. There was one of his mother, smiling, shimmering hair cascading to her shoulders, with a tall man in uniform, a cocky grin. Who was he? And more pictures of that soldier, without Teddy's mom, and him standing between older people with whom he shared a family resemblance.

"Who are these people?" Teddy had asked. "What do we do with all this stuff?"

Emily dug through a separate box, more slowly than Teddy. She stopped to skim letters, read yellowed clippings, documents.

"Look, it's your birth certificate!" She flapped it at him and then began to study it, at the same time placing a hand on her belly. He knew she was thinking about the certificate they'd soon be holding for their own child, seeing its name in print, the weight and length. She'd been smiling as she read, but her expression flattened. "Who's Theodore Jackson?"

He reached for the certificate. Impressed state seal, official paper. It showed his given name, his birth date, his mother's maiden name, McCray. But for father, instead of Henry Callison, it had this Jackson person. A common enough last name in the county, with claims of kinship to Thomas Jonathan "Stonewall" Jackson, but he'd never heard of a Theodore.

"It's a mistake," he said.

"Your folks would have noticed."

"A joke then. The real one must be in there somewhere."

"How did you survive this long without seeing your birth certificate?"

"No idea. My mom always took care of stuff like that." He pulled the box away from Emily—too roughly, he realized, so he patted her arm in apology—and started grabbing papers and shuffling through them. There was no other certificate.

As yet another explosion lit the sky, Emily struggled to her feet and approached the pregnant girl. Teddy couldn't hear what they were saying, but Emily pointed in his direction and the girl turned her head to look. She produced a pen from her bag, and the boy wrote on his hand, adding a temporary tattoo to his permanent collection.

"Her name's Tina," Emily said when she came back. "I invited them to the house tomorrow for the cookout."

"We don't know them, Em!"

"So? You keep telling me I need to meet more people. I'm meeting people."

"The guy's kind of cute," Tim said. "In a serial-killer kind of way."

Mysterious birth certificate in hand, Teddy and Emily had visited Aunt Irene. She served iced tea on the porch. Cicadas blared up and down the leafy street and the only breeze came from the funeral-parlor fan Irene waved in front of her face. Teddy knew Emily was miserable in the heat, but she sat where Irene had directed her and rocked.

His earliest memory of Irene was from that flood nearly 30 years earlier. His dad had handed him and his brother off to her and Uncle Marvin because the bridge was out, and he was going to try to get back to the farm. She was nervous then, Teddy remembered, moving knick-knacks to shelves out of his reach, fretting over how to entertain little boys in a house unspoiled by children, how to ease their anxiety about the rising river. Now, with her husband and brother both gone, she looked frail, disoriented. He wondered how long it would be until she could no longer care for herself, whether they'd need to move her out to the farm. That's what families did, wasn't it? But not if they sold the farm and moved into town, or back to Richmond. And then again, if the birth certificate was real, were they even family?

"Aunt Irene," Teddy began. He sipped his tea, felt condensation drip on his leg. It was too abrupt, he couldn't just spring it on her like that, so he backpedaled, spoke of the drought, of Tim, of the coming baby.

And then he couldn't put it off any longer.

"We were going through Dad's things." At the mention of her brother, Irene stopped waving the fan. "And we found something maybe you can explain."

The fan began to move again, slowly at first, then picking up speed.

"Who's Theodore Jackson?"

The fan stopped again. "More tea, dear?"

Teddy looked at Emily, then back at his aunt. The fan resumed. Emily's rocker creaked. A lawnmower roared across the street.

"Did you hear me, Irene?"

"I heard, dear."

"And?"

"I believe he was a friend of your mother's."

"Do you happen to know why this friend's name is on my birth certificate? In the place where it says, 'Name of Father?'"

"What do you want me to say, Teddy?"

"Tell me who he is."

Irene had dropped her fan to her lap. Her hand stroked the drooping, mottled skin of her neck. She gazed past him, as if toward the man in question.

"He was your mother's first husband." She took a deep breath. "Your father. He died before you were born."

There it was. A simple truth that changed everything. He grasped his glass with both hands. He lowered his gaze and spoke more to the scuffed gray paint of the porch than to his aunt.

"And no one ever thought to tell me this? About my own father?"

"Henry always loved you like a son, Teddy. They didn't want to upset things. He filed adoption papers as I recall. Told folks that you were named after his brother, but of course that wasn't quite true."

Irene's cat had joined them and slalomed through Teddy's legs before leaping to the porch rail.

"What was he like? Did he have family? Do I have cousins?"

"I barely knew him."

"Please. You must know something."

"I don't, Teddy. I'm sorry. But I know someone who might."

Teddy pulled up in front of the shack. He and Emily had driven deep into a hollow he'd never visited before, on a road he'd never heard of. The trees here, soaring sycamore and broad black walnut, cast lacy shadows on the scrabble yard and tin roof. They sat and waited. This was as close as he would ever come to his real father, and he wasn't sure what to do.

The screen door on the shack opened and a young man emerged.

"You folks lost?"

The voice was welcoming, the face smiling, and Teddy saw the man was barely more than a boy, with ruddy cheeks and flowing brown hair. He extended a hand as Teddy climbed out of the pick up.

"We're looking for Bobby Cabe," Teddy said, taking the boy's hand. Emily stayed put, only poking her head out the window when Teddy introduced her.

"That's me."

Teddy stared at the ramshackle house behind the boy, who couldn't be more than twenty. His eyes were chestnut, with flecks of yellow.

"But you probably want Bobby Senior," the boy said, his laughter filling the clearing. Then his grin faded. "This is his place, but he's not doing so hot."

The boy went inside and returned with an old man who barely made it outside before he plopped onto a bench on the porch. His breathing was labored, and he held a rag to his mouth as he coughed and spat.

"This is my father," the boy said. The old man nodded. His breath steadied.

A breeze swirled dust at Teddy's feet. He moved a step closer, saw the man wasn't so old. A scar creased his forehead above his right eye.

"We were told you might know something about a Theodore Jackson," Teddy said.

The man snorted and launched into another coughing fit.

"You mean Squirrel," he said, when the fit had passed. "I knew him. Weren't buddies or anything, but sure."

"Can you tell me about him?"

Cabe eyed Teddy and wiped his mouth with the rag. "You kin?"

"Looks that way," Teddy said.

"Thought so. Got the same jaw as him. Square. Nose, too."

"What happened to him?"

"Dead."

"How?"

Cabe peeked toward the truck at Emily. "Knifed," he said quietly.

The details came out haltingly, in one word answers to Teddy's impatient questioning. Squirrel had been popular in school, a football hero with a horndog reputation, swarmed by rumors of girls in trouble until the day he married Alice McCray, the one who wouldn't make the problem disappear, and shipped out to Vietnam. Not that being a newlywed changed his behavior. Bobby was never in Squirrel's league, never found the swagger, but in Saigon they were both small-town Virginia boys and made the rounds together, the bars, the Tu-do Street whore-houses.

"Squirrel was pissed one night because his girl was with some other grunt. Went crazy, jumped the guy, but it was Squirrel who took the blade."

"You saw this?"

"I did."

"And you didn't help him?" Teddy's face was hot, his voice loud.

He knew he sounded angry that this man had let his father die in a brawl over a whore, but he wasn't. How could he be? He didn't know Jackson, wasn't even born when he died, felt nothing for him now or ever, and, if the man had lived, Teddy's life would have been turned upside down. There'd have been no farm, no Tim, no Emily.

Cabe leaned away, eyes wide. "Hang on there, son. Nothing I could do. Don't take long to kill a man with the right knife. It was over fast."

Tina and Ben were the first to arrive for the cookout, and Baron, Teddy's father's arthritic mutt, trotted out to greet them. They were empty-handed, but Emily put Tina to work ferrying paper plates and plastic forks and cups from the kitchen to the tables she'd set up on the porch. Ben tagged along with Teddy to the grill, where the charcoal was refusing to light. Claiming talent with fires, he edged Teddy aside and took over. Teddy stepped back, folded his arms and watched the boy wield the lighter fluid and matches like a pro. He'd been reluctant to invite this odd young couple who would know no one and already seemed out of place. But Emily had a plan, she'd said, bold even by her standards of benign meddling. Tina and Ben weren't going to marry, Emily had learned, and Tina was too young and restless to raise the baby even if they did. There was no help forthcoming from their families, and Tina had her sights on school, a career. So adoption was on her mind. According to Emily, though, the girl hadn't yet made any arrangements, didn't really know where to begin, and, since the baby could arrive any day, time was of the essence. Emily knew of another couple in the area, Walt and Patsy, who desperately wanted a kid. They were expected at the cookout, too, and, after making the introductions, Emily—so she promised—would stay out of it. Where was the harm?

Except she'd also invited another family—Elton and Lucinda, who'd brought a baby home from China last Christmas—in case the other folks failed to take the hint. Teddy remembered the Asian toddler from the fireworks in the park and wondered what else Emily had schemed. Now that couple had arrived with their baby, an older woman in tow, and a couple of pies.

Another reminder of childhood. The pies brought back family baking marathons that drove him wild with anticipation. He and Tim, finished with Saturday chores, were commanded to wait on the porch while their mother and grandmother iced cakes, shaped cookies, cooled pies, until finally they were allowed to enter the kitchen and sample a slice of blueberry, his favorite, or a wedge of apple, Tim's.

Albert Haliwell and his kid DeShawn arrived next. Nephew, Teddy corrected himself. It couldn't be easy, even for a Sheriff's deputy like Al, to take a kid out of gang-plagued D.C. and drop him in the country in hopes he could avoid trouble. But trouble was everywhere. As he shuffled up the drive, the boy's hands were stuffed in his pockets, and he wouldn't look Teddy in the eye. It had been the same in court when Teddy, as a favor to Al, convinced Judge Hazlet that the fight DeShawn had been in was a simple misunderstanding, that he was a good kid defending himself from racist bullies. Or maybe it was Teddy who was uncomfortable around the boy, not having any idea what it took to keep a kid safe, not having any idea what it meant to raise a child. He sent DeShawn down to the pond to help Tim and thought he saw a smile on the boy's face at the prospect of the fireworks. Teddy watched Al as his eyes followed DeShawn.

And that made him think of Tim and kids. He'd be a terrific uncle. Would it matter that they didn't have the same father?

A new couple climbed out of a pickup. Walt and his wife, Teddy guessed. Emily had filled him in on their story—a troubled past for both, a miscarriage, a separation. She'd warned him not to offer either one a beer, but that looked not to be a problem, as they'd brought their own bottle of soda. The newcomers greeted Al Haliwell, and Teddy wondered what mischief had acquainted them with the Sheriff's department.

Next to show up, to Teddy's surprise, were Bobby Cabe and his

son, Bobby Jr. Teddy had no idea when Emily had invited them, or
why, except that the grizzled veteran was the only link to his real
father. Typical of Emily, doing what she thought was right for
everybody whether they liked it or not. But how was he supposed
to explain this hillbilly to Tim?

It was like the old days, with the clan gathered, the grill flaming
and fixings on the table, and Teddy felt like a kid, back in the house
where he grew up. Except his father wasn't there—either of his
fathers—his mom, his grandfather. He watched Emily and Tina
comparing their vast swells. Emily took that woman Patsy's hand
and placed it on Tina's belly, and they all laughed together. Walt
stood by the barbecue with young Ben, and both watched Al turn
the chicken pieces over the fire. Tim and the boy DeShawn trudged
up from the pond, their laughter preceding them. Even the Bobby
Cabes, father and son, appeared content to keep slow-moving Baron
occupied with a tennis ball.

As they consumed the meal—Teddy's mother's bean salad, a
recipe Emily had discovered among the cookbooks in the kitchen,
Aunt Irene brought a potato salad, and there were those pies—
Teddy tried to keep Tim from the Cabes and wrestled with what he
would tell him about his discovery. Chatter filled the porch, groaning
about over-indulgence, constant laughter.

"It's not a big deal," Emily said when they found themselves
alone for a moment. "Is it?"

"Maybe not," he said. "But everything's different now, with Dad
gone. Doesn't it seem like things are spinning out of control? He
was the glue." Teddy was thinking of his own uncertainty as much
as he was Tim's. "What's this going to do to us all?"

Teddy had not noticed its approach, but dusk was upon them.
Emily, with the help of Patsy and Tina, covered the leftovers and
moved them to the kitchen, and clusters of guests followed Tim
and DeShawn down to the pond: Irene with the Bobby Cabes,
Ben with Al Haliwell, Walt alongside Elton and Lucinda, carrying
their baby.

Even before everyone settled into the lawnchairs scattered at water's edge, Tim had launched the first salvo: a simple bottle rocket meant to announce the commencement of the festivities.

"They lied to us," Teddy imagined saying to Tim as he followed Emily and her new friends across the field. Just the beginning.

Tim fired a cluster of rockets that exploded in succession. The baby cried, or maybe that was DeShawn's delighted squeal.

"Our whole lives, we believed their lie," Teddy would say.

Tim crouched and lit a fuse, jogging back to where DeShawn stood with their munitions cache. Another explosion lit the sky, a backdrop of rainless clouds, and then the burst of red that opened, a flower in bloom that quickly faded.

"Red peony," said Tim, in his narrating voice.

"I thought I knew what I was passing on to my son," Teddy pictured himself saying. "He was going to be the scion of a great family that settled in this valley two centuries ago. But who is he now? Where does he belong?"

A blue explosion flared, followed by the crackling guns. DeShawn and Tim shuttled between their supplies and the launch pad. A whistling green-tailed missile, then a swirling dance of yellow, orange and red. Then the dense silver sun Teddy recalled from the park. Then the golden willow, with its long, delicate branches.

DeShawn and Tim bent to set up new rockets, lit the fuses and ran. The smoke trail for one rose straight up, but the other veered. A yellow peony blossomed in the same vicinity as the previous explosions, but its red twin seemed just above their heads. A collective gasp erupted. Sparks rained, and Emily—Teddy thought it was Emily, but everyone was scrambling out of harm's way and he couldn't be sure—shrieked. Another rocket screamed skyward and burst, and in the glow of this new explosion Teddy saw smoke rising from the top of the old sycamore on the ridge. When the light faded, the flames materialized among the high, dry leaves: feeble at first, uncertain, but in seconds they gained confidence and spread.

With the immediate threat of sparks passed, the guests, now standing, watched the tree. Emily slipped next to Teddy, wrapped an arm around him.

"Is there anything we can do?" she asked.

"I don't know," he said. It was a handsome fire, like a candle against the horizon that illuminated the slope, the barren rock, the silvery brush, casting long shadows.

"It's almost Biblical," she said. "A sign."

"Right," he said. "Sure." Tim was watching the tree now, too. He turned to look at Teddy, as if asking for advice, like when they were kids. Teddy shrugged.

"Sign or not," Emily said, "don't you think this is a good time to talk to him?"

The burning tree was alive, with the flames still spreading, smoke tumbling skyward, embers falling through the twisted branches. Emily nudged Teddy forward. He gave the tree a last look and stepped through the dry grass. Tim stood at the edge of the pond, as if the water would somehow rise up and quench the fire, and Teddy was drawn to the dreamy reflection of the flames on the still surface. The sound of the crackling leaves came to him, distant, with the rustling of worried voices, now backing away toward the safety of the house.

But Teddy could not take his eyes from the image of the tree in the water, the great burning flower of his youth.

CLIFFORD GARSTANG grew up in the Midwest and received a BA from Northwestern University. After serving as a Peace Corps Volunteer in South Korea, he earned an MA in English and a JD, both from Indiana University, and practiced international law in Singapore, Chicago, and Los Angeles with one of the largest law firms in the United States. Subsequently, he earned an MPA in International Development from Harvard University's John F. Kennedy School of Government and worked for Harvard Law School as a legal reform consultant in Almaty, Kazakhstan. From 1996 to 2001, he was Senior Counsel for East Asia at the World Bank in Washington, D.C., where his work concentrated on China, Indonesia and Vietnam.

Garstang received an MFA in Creative Writing from Queens University of Charlotte in 2003. His work has appeared in *Virginia Quarterly Review*, *Shenandoah*, *The Ledge*, *The Baltimore Review*, *North Dakota Quarterly*, *Potomac Review* and elsewhere, and has received Distinguished Mention in the Best American Series. He won the 2006 *Confluence* Fiction Prize and the 2007 *GSU Review* Fiction Prize and is a Fellow of the Virginia Center for the Creative Arts.

He currently lives in the Shenandoah Valley of Virginia.

About the Cover Artist

BOB MILLER entered the international scene of photography in 2005. His pictures have been viewed by over a million people worldwide on his Flickr Website. He specializes in nature and landscape. His unique style has earned him the respect of noted photographers across the globe.

He has been most noted for his landscape and wildlife photography on the Blue Ridge Parkway. His photographs have appeared in many publications worldwide, and other forms of media including movies, calendars, and projected images in classical concerts in Italy.

Some of his publications include *National Geographic, JPG Magazine, Image Driven Magazine, In the Moment* (an Australian Arts Publication) and local *Central Virginia*. He has won both national and local awards for his photography. Most recently he won second place in the National Parks Foundation "Share the Experience" photo contest (2008). In 2007 and 2008, he placed first in the John Faber Smith Mountain Arts Council photo contest.

His photography has been displayed in galleries around the world from France to Switzerland. In Switzerland his photographs were featured in the Musee de l'Elysee the largest photography museum in the world. His photographs have been collected and appreciated by best selling authors, artists, and some of the most famous photographers around the world.

He has published three photography books: *The Blue Ridge and Beyond, Visual Destination: The Blue Ridge Parkway,* and *Dirt Track Racing.*

Author's Note

I'd like to thank Kevin Watson of Press 53, without whom this book would not exist. Working with him has been a terrific experience.

Thanks also to Fred Leebron and Michael Kobre for creating the fabulous MFA Program at Queens University of Charlotte, where I learned how much I needed to learn, and a big thank you to all of the faculty and my peers in the program who aided in that discovery with their insightful instruction and criticism.

Special thanks to Mary Akers, a good friend and amazing writer, who helped all of the stories in this collection progress through multiple drafts; her contribution has been immeasurable.

The faculty and participants of the Sewanee Writers' Conference, Bread Loaf Writers' Conference, Indiana University Writers' Conference, and Under the Volcano Master Classes also helped shape many of these stories, and for that I'm exceedingly grateful. Thanks also to the Virginia Center for the Creative Arts for providing the time and space to write, and to the many artists I have come to know there over the years who have been so supportive. I also am indebted to the Zoetrope Virtual Studio and to my fellow writers there for maintaining such a warm and congenial creative community.

Finally, to my family and friends, thanks for the unequivocal encouragement when I decided to leave the old life behind.

CG

Breinigsville, PA USA
14 March 2010
234150BV00001B/3/P